"How did you survive the ride with all that noise?"

"Found my happy place." Jalissa loosened Flo and moved back so the dog could exit the van through the driver's side.

"You know what happiness is?" Rider smirked.

"Hardy har-har." Jalissa rounded the back to start unloading the animals. "Where am I putting them?"

"Oh, don't worry about it. The guys already know where everything is set up."

"Then I can leave?" She had a load of laundry she could do.

"Oh, no." He tsked at her. "We need your assistance with the animals."

Jalissa slowly inched backward but stopped when Flo nudged her. *One…two…* She could do this. Be near the firehouse. She didn't actually have to go *inside*, did she? Flo licked her fingertips.

"All right," Jalissa said. "I'll just stay out of everyone's way unless I'm needed."

"You'll be needed." He stared into her eyes.

She blinked slowly. What was going on with her? First thinking Rider was good-looking, and now they were having some kind of moment. She needed to fix this real quick.

Toni Shiloh is a wife, mom and multipublished Christian contemporary romance author. She writes to bring God glory and to learn more about His goodness. A member of the American Christian Fiction Writers (ACFW) and of the Virginia Chapter, Toni loves connecting with readers via social media. You can learn more about her at tonishiloh.com.

Books by Toni Shiloh

Love Inspired

An Unlikely Proposal
An Unlikely Alliance

Visit the Author Profile page at LoveInspired.com.

An Unlikely Alliance

Toni Shiloh

LOVE INSPIRED

INSPIRATIONAL ROMANCE

LOVE INSPIRED®

INSPIRATIONAL ROMANCE

Recycling programs
for this product may
not exist in your area.

ISBN-13: 978-1-335-58508-0

An Unlikely Alliance

Love Inspired
22 Adelaide St. West, 41st Floor
Toronto, Ontario M5H 4E3, Canada
www.LoveInspired.com

Printed in U.S.A.

Casting all your care upon him;
for he careth for you.
—*1 Peter* 5:7

To the Author and Finisher of my faith.

Acknowledgments

There are so many people I would love to thank for helping this book go from idea to published novel. I'd love to thank my critique partner Sarah Monzon for helping me improve this story. I appreciate you more than words can say!

A special thanks to Jessica Shevy for naming The Beanery.

I'd love to thank the Love Inspired team. Thank you to Dina Davis for your awesome editing skills. Also, I'd love to thank the art team, marketing and everyone else who made this story come to life. Thanks for making writing enjoyable!

Last but not least, I'd like to thank my husband and kids. Glenn, thank you for encouraging me in my writing. Thank you to my kids for listening to me talk about titles and everything else book related. I love y'all so much!

Chapter One

Jalissa Tucker stormed through the double doors of the community center where the Bluebonnet town hall was taking place. If the mayor thought she'd sit back quietly while the city cut her funding—dooming the animal rescue shelter to go out of business—he had another think coming. She slipped into a vacant seat toward the back while the mayor droned on about the order of business. So much for arriving late enough to miss this monotonous part and get right to the heart of the matter. *Oh, well.*

She scanned the open room, surprised at how many of the townspeople had come out. Jalissa jerked back in her seat as her gaze slammed into the form of Jeremy Rider. *Ugh.* That man was like a splinter. He made subtle digs that got under her skin and wouldn't budge no matter how much she tugged. Since her best friend had married Rider's friend, she saw way too much of the annoying man.

He had to be here for some specific reason, though. Maybe he'd come in an official role, checking to ensure the attendees didn't surpass the building's capacity limit. Although he wasn't wearing the Bluebonnet Fire Department uniform, he'd probably come in that vein.

What other reason would bring Rider to a town hall meeting?

"In regard to the town budget, we will be reducing funds or completely defunding certain programs due to a limited amount of resources. Unfortunately, the Parks and Recreation program is in that purview. Funding will be halved, and all requests for new equipment or new programs will require prior council approval." The mayor paused. "Any objections?"

Jalissa wanted to object on behalf of Bluebonnet's youth, but she really needed to conserve her energy and voice for the animal shelter. Yesterday she'd learned their usual yearly grant had been denied. If the mayor removed city funding, then Jalissa would be left at the mercy of what little donors remained. Alas, their contributions wouldn't cover the shelter's expenses, which meant she'd be forced to cut employee hours, and eventually employees themselves, until she'd have no choice but to close the shelter doors. Not to mention the worry of what would happen to the precious animals. She couldn't let them be displaced. Her employees could always find another job, but tracking down another no-kill shelter to take the dogs and cats would be difficult.

When no one spoke up, the mayor continued. "Moving right along." He listed two other programs that would have their funding restricted. A few people objected, and he overruled them but ensured the secretary noted their complaints.

Jalissa rolled her eyes. What was the point of objecting if the mayor wouldn't actually hear the reasons behind people's complaints? She'd come here to stop them from removing the shelter's funding, not to become some footnote in the city memo. Was this how every town hall worked in Bluebonnet, Texas? She'd never been to one before—had really never seen a reason to attend.

"All righty, now, next up is Bluebonnet Animal Rescue."

She straightened in her seat, clutching her purse strap close to her chest.

"The town can no longer afford to fund the shelter. There aren't enough folks adopting the pets to defray the cost of operations. The city will henceforth cut all funding."

She sucked in a breath, trying to scramble for air at the awful pronouncement. *One...two...*

"Any objections?" The mayor scanned the crowd.

Three... Jalissa jumped to her feet. "I object!"

"Of course you do, Ms. Tucker." Mayor Douglas heaved a sigh, whipping his glasses off to rub at his eyes. "Kate, make a note of Jalissa's objections. Moving along to the SAFE program. Regrettably, it will also be defunded."

"Wait just a minute," Jalissa started.

"I object," Rider shouted.

She whirled toward Rider, who stood on the other side of the aisle. "You can't object to my objection."

"Actually, Ms. Tucker," Mayor Douglas interrupted, "he can."

"But I wasn't," Rider said smoothly. He folded his arms across his chest. "My objection is for defunding SAFE. The teens in Bluebonnet need the antibullying program. Having mentors ensures they can navigate the trials of life with someone walking alongside them. We don't want to isolate our teens, Mr. Mayor."

"Wait a minute." Jalissa held up a hand, momentarily stunned that Rider cared about anything other than himself. Who knew the cocky firefighter had a heart? She turned back to the mayor. "I'm not done with my objection."

"Ms. Tucker, I noted it, and we're moving right along." Mayor Douglas peered over the rim of his glasses to stare at Rider. "And we'll note your objection as well, Mr. Rider."

"So that's it?" Rider asked. "You aren't actually going to do anything about it?"

"Exactly." Jalissa resisted the urge to stomp her foot. "What's the point of a town hall meeting if you won't hear what the *town* has to say, Mr. Mayor?"

"As stated at the *very* beginning—" he pierced her with his gaze "—objections will be noted, then discussed at the end. But since you two seem intent on disrupting the order, please tell me what, exactly, you want me to do? I can't make money grow on trees or rub a magic lamp," he groused.

Oops. Guess she should've made it to the beginning of the meeting, but evidently, neither had Rider. Jalissa drew in a steady breath, fighting for calm and composure before speaking. Her insides quaked as she searched for the right words.

"Mr. Mayor, wouldn't it be better to come up with a different idea to keep these programs funded that won't overtax the city budget?"

"Do you think you can come up with a better idea than our *accountant*?" His bushy brows furrowed like caterpillars burrowing into a cocoon. He directed a pointed stare in her direction. "He's the one who made the recommended cuts. He looked at the numbers and presented me with the list I'm introducing to everyone now."

"There has to be a better way, Mr. Mayor," Rider added. "I'm with Jalissa. You can't leave these programs with no assistance whatsoever. It won't help the youth who need SAFE or, in her case—" he hooked a finger her way "—help abandoned animals." A spark glinted in his eye. "Although, I think it would be better to help the teens and let the animals figure out their own way."

"You would," she muttered. Animals were more defenseless than people. Sometimes it felt like she was the only one fighting for them.

Rider smirked, as if he could tell how much he'd irked her.

A hand shot up from the front row, and Mrs. Baker, the owner of the local bookstore, stood. "What about some kind of fund-raiser? Would that help?"

"Yes." Jalissa clapped. "Great idea, Mrs. Baker. There's your alternative, Mr. Mayor." She sat down, watching an array of emotions cross the mayor's face.

"I don't have time for a fund-raiser," he muttered.

"Well, neither do I," said Mrs. Baker. "But it *is* a solution."

Mr. Douglas peered over the rims of his eyeglasses and out into the crowd. "How many of you here want to object to a program that's being defunded or having funds reduced?"

Hands shot up around the room.

"Fine, then. I'll talk to our accountant and see if we can put a hold on this for a little bit longer. Give y'all time to do a fund-raiser."

"Who's y'all?" Rider asked.

"Why, you and Ms. Tucker, of course." The mayor smirked. "Y'all wanted another way, you've got one. You two will be the official fund-raising committee. Keep in mind, we can't finance your fund-raising efforts. What you raise will go directly to the six programs listed today."

"Wait a minute, sir," Rider said. "If Jalissa and I are doing all the work, shouldn't the majority of the funds go to the animal shelter and SAFE?"

Mayor Douglas pursed his lips. "If your fund-raising efforts are minimal, then yes, I can agree to that arrangement. However, if it's enough to fund more than your two programs, I believe it should benefit the town as a whole. Meeting adjourned."

Jalissa felt her mouth drop, stunned by the bizarre turn of events. What had started out as a crusade to keep her job and save the animals had now turned into her worst nightmare: working with a firefighter. And not just any firefighter, but *Jeremy Rider*.

Jeremy Rider wanted to stop the mayor's retreat from the community center and ask what crime he'd committed to be punished with the likes of Jalissa Tucker, the woman who hated him, for some unknown reason, which was ironic, since *he* had every reason to dislike *her*. He remembered all the times she'd stood by silently as the popular crowd at their high school—aka *her* friends—made his teenage life miserable. He'd been overweight, awkward and everything a teen boy didn't want to be. Not to mention Jalissa had no idea how to relax and have a little bit of fun. Her default setting stayed pricklier than a cactus spine.

Since he'd started hanging out with the Youngs, and, by extension, her, she'd gotten worse. Which was odd, because that's when he and Omar Young had finally settled into an easy friendship. When Rider had first started working at the Bluebonnet Fire Department, he'd had a bad habit of joking at inopportune times that others, including Omar, didn't always find amusing. Rider enjoyed bringing levity to a situation, though not everyone appreciated his brand of humor.

But with Jalissa, he had no idea if his personality stuck in her craw or if something else bothered her. 'Course, she could simply be a man hater. He'd never seen her date anyone, and she seemed to avoid firefighters like the latest plague. Seemed she preferred animal companionship over human—she usually had her dog with her—probably because they couldn't talk back.

He meandered across the aisle and sat backward on the seat facing her. Her fingers flew across her cell phone screen, so he took a moment to catalog her features. Her long brown hair had been parted in the middle and hung in straight lines, brushing her shoulders. He couldn't see her eyes, but he knew they were brown, just a tad darker than her skin and a richer color than her hair.

Rider cleared his throat. "Looks like we're the fundraising committee."

She lifted her head and rolled her eyes. "Puh-lease. I can't work with you."

Exhibit A. He raised an eyebrow and waited for her to spew whatever venom she had for him today.

"You're not going to say anything?" Her arms folded across her chest.

"What's there to say? You don't want to work with me, don't." He shrugged. "But the animal shelter shouldn't receive some of the funds if I have to do all the work myself."

She gasped. "You wouldn't dare."

"Look, if you want your program to benefit from the fund-raiser, then you'll cochair with me like the mayor said. Otherwise, I'll find someone else to help." Though whom, he had no idea. The community center had quickly cleared out.

Jalissa snorted. "In your dreams. Everyone's just going to say we were already tasked—" She bit her bottom lip, brow furrowing with irritation.

"That's because we were." He wanted to smirk at how her spine stiffened with the admission.

She couldn't argue—although he was pretty sure she was about to burst from suppressing her desire to do so—since he merely stated facts.

"Maybe," she started slowly, "we should talk this over. How about we go over to the Beanery?"

Rider glanced around. "That's fine."

They parted ways in the community center's parking lot, and Rider hopped into his truck as Jalissa got into a hatchback that had seen better days.

By the time he walked into the Beanery, his nerves were amped and his mind had spun different scenarios on how working with Jalissa could go. While he assumed she'd have a difficult time pairing up with him, Rider didn't know if he could survive her company, either. Although she'd never specifically joined in the taunts of his childhood, he couldn't forgive her for just standing there.

What had gone on in her mind that made her choose silence back then? She certainly had a lot to say these days. He took in a deep breath, inhaling the aromatic scent of coffee, and pushed aside his ruminations. Out of all the places in Bluebonnet, the coffee shop was his favorite. They kept the music low enough to carry on a conversation and high enough to soften the atmosphere.

Not that he noticed details like that.

He strolled up to the counter, thankful no one else was in line. "Hey, Tiff. Can I get the usual?" The dark roast made by Colombian Brew was his favorite. "Oh, could I also get a marble brownie?" No telling how long the conversation with Jalissa would go, and he needed something to tide him over before his shift started at the firehouse. One of the guys would be on meal duty, but Rider had a high metabolism that had him reaching for food all throughout the day.

Once more his thoughts turned to Jalissa. Would she tone down the animosity even a little in order to work with him? Could *he* ignore the old hurt that was present whenever she was near? The people at SAFE needed him to act mature. Plus, he didn't know the first thing about fundraising. Putting out fires? Yes. Saving cats for old ladies? Oddly enough, not as cliché as most people thought. Raising money so SAFE would be able to continue the ministry of reaching out to hurting teens? Yeah, not a clue. But if he had to put up with Jalissa's temperamental attitude to secure funding for SAFE, he would.

Help me help SAFE, Lord.

A barista called his name, and Rider grabbed his drink and food, then strolled to the back of the Beanery. He liked to be tucked in the corner, where he could watch the patrons in front of him. Which was how he saw Jalissa as soon as she walked in. She scanned the room and visibly jolted when her gaze landed on him.

Lord, help me not make her mad. He'd be lying if he claimed to not enjoy getting under her skin. Sometimes, he wanted to know what would aggravate her the most. Other times, he prayed they could remain civil enough to get through an entire conversation. Which was his prayer right now.

Jalissa sank into the chair opposite him, and Rider reached for a calm he didn't feel.

"You didn't want to get a drink?" he asked.

"No, let's just get this over with."

He bit back a sigh.

"First off, I'll work with you as long as you're civil."

He pointed to his chest. "*Me?* Don't you mean *you*?"

She arched an eyebrow. "And don't act like you know everything or think you're some precious gift to humanity."

"Hey, pot, did you forget you're the kettle?" He gripped his coffee cup. It was so easy for her to push the blame on someone else.

"And no jokes." She waved a hand in the air as if he hadn't even spoken. "They're not funny, and I only feel pity when you try."

Ouch. That jab actually hurt. His uncle told him all the time how funny he was. Telling jokes was the only way Rider knew how to break the ice. Did other people think his jokes fell flat? *No.* He could remember numerous times people had laughed. Maybe Jalissa was deflecting.

Rider stared at her. "You done?"

"For now."

"Good." He leaned forward. "I have some stipulations of my own."

She arched an eyebrow. "Like what?"

"One, you tone down the animosity. It's bad enough I could get burned at work. I don't need to be scorched by you."

Color drained out of her face, and she stood, her chair screeching backward at the abrupt movement. He reached for her arm but stopped before he touched her and held up his hands instead. "Please, I have no idea what I did, but I wasn't trying to be rude." Not this time, at least. The wounded look in her eye was reminiscent of the scars he'd carried from high school. He might like to spar with words, but he never actually intended to inflict a wound.

"Forget about it," she snapped.

"Are we good?" He gestured toward her empty seat.

She sank into the chair. "I'll work with you, if that's what you're asking."

In other words, they'd never be best friends. He could live with that. "Great. I'm going on shift today. Maybe we could meet when I get off tomorrow?"

"Don't you need sleep?" she eyed him skeptically.

"Yeah, but I also don't want to waste time. The teens at SAFE are depending on me."

She eyed him as if searching for his sincerity. He waited silently. She could either believe him or not.

"Text me when you're off shift."

"May I have your number?" He handed her his unlocked phone.

She rolled her eyes, but her fingers flew across the screen, putting her info into his contacts. "There. Are we done now?"

He sighed, exhausted by her attitude. "Yes, Jalissa. Talk to you Wednesday." Maybe then they'd both be in a better mood and able to work for the good of Bluebonnet.

Chapter Two

Jalissa pulled the lever that pushed her car seat forward so Flo could jump out of the back. "Come on, girl."

The golden retriever sniffed the air as Jalissa manually locked the door. She clicked her tongue twice, and Flo fell into a trot beside her as they strolled toward the park bench where Jalissa's friend Trinity Young waited.

"Hey, Trinity." Jalissa sat down. Flo circled around before coming to a rest.

"Hey, girl." Trinity rubbed her pregnant belly.

Jalissa's best friend was only four months pregnant, but her belly had bloomed as if she were at least six months along. Jalissa searched the playground and spotted Trinity's two stepdaughters swinging.

"How are you?" Trinity asked.

"Ugh, I'll tell you later." Jalissa pointed to Trinity's stomach. "How are you and the little one?"

A huge smile lit Trinity's face. "I think I felt him move today."

Jalissa gasped. "It's a boy?"

"I have no idea." Trinity grinned. "I just have a feeling." She bit her lip. "I do try not to say *he* so much in case I'm wrong."

"And you still don't want to find out?" Jalissa couldn't fathom it.

"No. I like the anticipation of not knowing."

Jalissa shook her head. "The suspense would do me in. How do you know what to buy if you don't know the sex of the baby?"

"Like every mom before technology ruined the surprise, you purchase neutral colors. Besides, my mom will buy a lot of clothes once the baby is born."

"I suppose." Jalissa didn't want to buy only light yellows, especially if the baby was a girl. Wasn't part of the fun in shopping being able to select cute dresses if it was a girl or overalls for a boy? She stared out at the park, watching the trees rustle from the wind, and squeezed the bridge of her nose. "So, the reason why I wanted to meet you today was to talk about yesterday's town hall meeting."

"How'd that go?"

"Miserable!" The word burst out of her. "The mayor told me to work with Rider on some made-up fund-raising committee. Which, of course, I have no desire to do. I mean, the arrogance on that man is ridiculous. Rider is *so* annoying."

Flo's ears pricked as if sensing Jalissa's stifled inward scream. She rose to her haunches and placed her head in Jalissa's lap.

"I take it you're frustrated," Trinity said, mirth curving her mouth upward.

Jalissa stroked Flo's soft fur, letting the action soothe her. "That's an understatement."

"Does that mean the mayor isn't cutting funding?"

Jalissa took her time explaining the fiasco that had been the town hall meeting, this time with more calm and less bitterness, although the emotions still sat in her gut like a bomb waiting to go off.

"What are you going to do?" Trinity asked.

"We're meeting once he gets off shift." Just thinking about his job made her stomach contents want to erupt. She placed a hand to her middle, trying to concentrate on breathing.

Flo nudged Jalissa's hand. *One...two...*

Firefighters couldn't be trusted to get the job done right. Sure, they ran into burning buildings, but did they rescue every person in need? No. Too often they made the calculated choice of one person over another, leaving death in their wake and victims six feet under. Victims like her father.

Three...four...five...

Jalissa willed the tears to fade as she scratched behind the golden retriever's silky ears. The repetitive strokes loosened the band around her chest and made her cognizant of the shallow breaths she'd begun taking. She drew in a deep well of oxygen and exhaled slowly as she restarted her count to ten. Though Flo didn't have her emotional support vest on, her companion stepped into her training without its prompting.

"Can you handle working with him, Jalissa? I know he kind of gets under your skin," Trinity said softly.

Jalissa shrugged, feigning nonchalance. Though Trinity knew Jalissa's anxiety struggles, Jalissa had no wish to voice all of them right now. Instead, she went with the inevitable. "I have to." The petulant tone of her voice managed to reach her own ears. She sounded like Trinity's stepdaughters when given something they didn't like to eat and told to clean their plates.

Jeremy Rider certainly embodied that one piece of broccoli on Jalissa's dish. She'd just have to remember that keeping herself and the shelter employees employed—not to mention caring for the helpless animals—was worth the intense displeasure of his company.

"Mommy!" Trinity's youngest stepdaughter came running. She held her finger outstretched, her rounded cheeks covered with tear streaks.

"What's wrong, sweetie?" Trinity bent over Joy's hand, cradling it in her own.

"Owie." Joy sniffed.

"Oh, she has a splinter," Trinity murmured.

Jalissa watched as her friend pulled some tweezers from

the large tote Trinity had been carrying since she'd married the widower. With Omar working the firefighter shift of twenty-four hours on and twenty-four hours off, Trinity had bonded easily with the children, and they now called her Mommy.

A twinge of envy filtered through Jalissa, but she pushed the emotions away. She'd rather be alone than end up a widow with kids to raise without a father. She couldn't risk a repeat of her childhood. No child should have their father ripped from their arms and see the grief that aged their mother faster than time itself.

Rodney Tucker had enjoyed a simple yet honorable life. Jalissa had been the epitome of a daddy's girl, and her heart had never been the same once he'd passed.

She missed him terribly.

Thankfully, the Tucker side of the family kept his memory alive. They celebrated his birthdays and shared their favorite memories at family functions. Unfortunately, her mother's side of the family had shunned Jalissa's mother for marrying an African American. Mr. and Mrs. Perez—what Jalissa called the grandparents she'd never met—had thought life would be unbearable for her mother if she married a Black man. Although Jalissa had experienced racism, knowing her grandparents wanted nothing to do with her because of her father's heritage hurt the worst.

She gave a mental shake of the head. Despite her love for her firefighter father, she would not date a man who wore a uniform. And she would definitely never, *ever* date a firefighter. They left behind heartache, turning women into widows and children into orphans. Every important milestone of Jalissa's had been met with an ache at her father's absence. All because some ladderman decided to break ranks and left her father to fight a fire by himself.

Hence the reason all firemen were removed from her

dating pool. For added precaution, Jalissa eliminated other first responders and military members as well.

Her eyes shifted, watching the scene before her. Trinity wrapped Joy's finger in a bandage and kissed the little girl on the cheek. The preschooler grinned, wiped her tears, then raced to the playground once more.

Trinity sighed as she leaned back against the seat. "I hope the fund-raiser works. It would be a shame to lose the shelter or any of the other programs."

"Agreed." But a selfish part of Jalissa wanted to save the animal shelter more than the others. Animals, always ready to bestow affection and give loyalty to their owners, were the biggest part of her life. She'd be lost without Flo and her support on the days it seemed like anxiety won.

However, Jalissa couldn't simply discount the other programs, either. Everyone in Bluebonnet believed in a cause special to them.

She turned to Trinity. "Hey, did you know Rider volunteered with SAFE?" She was still shocked by the idea of him mentoring a teen.

Trinity shook her head. "I had no idea."

"Hmm." That one piece of information didn't fit with all she knew about the man.

"I'll be praying God guides you," Trinity said, squeezing Jalissa's arm.

She nodded stiffly. *Thanks, but prayer isn't necessary.* The whole fund-raising business wasn't that big of a deal. Surely Jalissa could handle this on her own and save the big-ticket items for God to focus on. How would He feel if she annoyed Him for every little thing? No, Mamí had taught her that hard work would garner success. Jalissa didn't want to be someone who sat and did nothing, expecting God to show up like some genie.

Besides, Jalissa had all she needed to succeed—the

affections of Flo, the support of her best friend and an attitude that could keep an egotistical firefighter in check.

Rider set his duffel bag on the seat and closed the cab of his truck. He hopped in the driver's seat and let out a sigh when his head touched the headrest. He had a few hours before his meeting with Jalissa. Although his shift ended at noon, Jalissa couldn't leave the shelter until four. She apparently had a lunch appointment already scheduled.

For now, he'd stop by the SAFE center and check in on his pal Sean. The program was essential for Bluebonnet's teens, giving them a mentor to talk to about life and, more specifically, bullying. Ever since the coordinator had announced the possibility of the city shutting them down, Sean had been a ball of anxiety. Rider had promised no matter what, he'd be there for the teen.

Belinda—the SAFE coordinator—was responsible for matching adults with the kids who had been bullied or sought help personally. She'd been near tears when she heard about the city's proposed defunding, and Rider had quickly volunteered to attend the town hall to ease her burden. He wouldn't be the man he was today if it wasn't for the mentorship that had helped him when he was younger. His uncle had been a big factor in shaping Rider. Uncle Jay had instilled values in Rider while teaching him how to handle the constant bullying. He'd even inspired Rider to become a firefighter.

Knowing other kids weren't so fortunate to have a male figure in their lives, Rider had reached out to Belinda to sign up as a SAFE mentor. When he'd been matched with Sean, suddenly the depth of his commitment challenged him. Going up against a four-alarm fire seemed safer than all the hurt and anger that had been bottled inside the fourteen-year-old. After much prayer, Rider stuck with it. Spending time with Sean and doing the SAFE activities

Belinda organized had allowed them to reach a truce and even develop a genuine friendship.

Rider parked his truck, then headed inside. The SAFE center brimmed with activity. He waved to the teens playing board games. Others played video games, oblivious to their surroundings. They shouted out directions to one another, headphones clearly keeping them from noticing how loudly they spoke.

Rider walked to the check-in partition and signed his name in the logbook.

"How did the town hall go?" Nessa asked.

Rider studied the surly teenager. "Hey, Nessa. Nice to see you, too."

She rolled eyes rimmed in black eyeliner. "Whatever, Rider. How did it go?"

He leaned his elbow against the partition, letting his body weight rest on the strength of his arm. "Unexpectedly."

"That, like, literally tells me nothing." She clutched the partition, attempting to bore a hole in his heart with her stare.

Nessa's glares were oddly effective for a teen, but Rider knew she had a heart of gold. "Sorry, kiddo. I need to talk to Belinda before I can say anything else."

"Fine." She blew out a breath and turned to knock on the closed door behind her.

"Come in," Belinda called.

Nessa cracked the door open. "Rider's got news about the meeting and won't tell me how it went."

"Tell him to come in."

Rider opened the lower partition, making sure the check-in log didn't jostle from the raised countertop. He closed the door behind him, then walked to Belinda's office. "Thanks, squirt."

"Please stop calling me that. It's Nessa."

"Right, squirt." He winked then headed into Belinda's office.

"Have a seat, and feel free to close the door so Nessa can stop eavesdropping."

"I heard that!"

"My point exactly," Belinda yelled back.

Rider chuckled and did as instructed. He sat down on the threadbare chair in front of Belinda's small desk, both of which had seen better days. The center ran completely on donations and what little of the city budget they were allotted, so everything was secondhand. Maybe Rider should do a fund-raiser to get updated furniture for the center as well.

"Please tell me you convinced the mayor to reverse his decision?" Crinkles creased around Belinda's worry-filled blue eyes.

"Kind of."

"What does that mean?" She nibbled on the end of her pencil, her gray hair hanging lifeless around her shoulders.

"It means he gave me and Jalissa Tucker the task of creating a fund-raiser. We've gotta come up with ways to make more money to save all the programs on the chopping block, though SAFE and the shelter will get first crack at the funds." He rubbed his chin, barely noting the stubble.

"How are y'all supposed to do that?" She flopped back against her chair, dropping the pencil.

"I'm meeting with Jalissa in a couple of hours to brainstorm." And hopefully her heart would grow a couple of sizes to ease her bite. Life would be easier if she played nice.

"Wow. I really appreciate you going down there. I've been slammed with all this paperwork." Belinda motioned to the piles of paper littering her desk.

"I'm happy to help. Really, you know how much this place means to me."

"I do." The lines around her mouth softened as she pushed her hair from her face.

He noted the wrinkles on her hands and the tense way she kept opening and closing her fist. Belinda needed an assistant, but the funds just weren't there. The least he could do was go to a town hall meeting.

He said as much.

"Thank you so much, Rider."

"Is Sean in today?" Rider hadn't made any plans to meet with his pal since he had been on shift, but if Sean was already at SAFE, Rider would make the time to hang out.

"No. Why? Were you supposed to meet?"

"No, no. Just checking." He stood and headed for the door, which was literally two steps away. Belinda's office had likely been a closet at some point. "See you later."

"Keep me updated."

"I will." But first, he had to make it through his meeting with Jalissa.

The irony of the whole situation rose up. He was supposed to work with a woman who had never stood up for him when her friends degraded him in the view of hundreds of their classmates. He had to work with someone like that to save a program that gave kids a safe place from bullying. *God, sometimes life really is hilarious.*

But his laughter was chock-full of sarcasm—not a speck of happiness in sight. Rider didn't want to have to fake niceness or wait for the proverbial shoe to drop. *Please, Lord, make a way in an impossible situation.* Because the last twenty-four hours of what-ifs had drained him.

He ran a hand through his hair after exiting Belinda's office. Scanning the premises, he noted the joy on the teens' faces. This. This was what he was fighting for. If that meant working with Jalissa, then so be it. SAFE was worth any hassle she threw his way.

Chapter Three

One...two...three...

Jalissa slowly counted as she rubbed Flo's back. Counting, combined with the slow movements of petting her dog, melted her anxiety like ice on hot asphalt. Something about the two erased tension from her mind—until her imagination spun up again when she realized she'd have to meet Rider in half an hour.

She'd spent the morning brainstorming ideas for fundraising, even asking the volunteers and shelter employees for their thoughts. Hopefully, the prep work would make the time with Rider go smoothly. Too bad he was such an unknown variable. He claimed she was the one with the issue, but she wasn't the first to fire a snarky comment then turn around and call it a joke.

Four...five...

Flo's head shifted on her knee as if the goldie could sense that counting was failing Jalissa. Her nerves spiked with frustration as her heartbeat increased and her hands began to tremble. *Why can't I calm down?*

Years of watching her mother manage multiple jobs after her father's passing and take care of Jalissa's anxiety issues had built a need for independence. Papí would have hated to see her mother work so hard, but firefighter death benefits hadn't been enough to live on.

She hadn't wanted to add to Mamí's burden, so at eighteen, she'd moved out of their tiny apartment so her mother could quit the extra jobs and focus on housekeeping. A few years later, Jalissa had rescued Flo from the shelter, and the dog had been designated as an emotional support animal by her psychiatrist. Flo had helped Jalissa gain confidence in her independence.

Still, there were days like today, when life didn't go as planned.

The need for control was one reason she was determined to come up with the best fund-raising ideas. She would prove her worth and show Rider how indispensable she was. Bonus points if he realized she didn't need him.

Six...seven...eight...

Everything will work out for good.

Jalissa checked the time on her cell, then rose to her feet. "Bed, Flo."

Flo trotted over to the open crate and twirled in a circle before lying on the dog pillow. The dog was getting older and took more time to relax into a position of rest these days. Jalissa shifted the lock into place and whispered, "Goodbye." She grabbed her purse, notebook and keys. If she just kept repeating, *everything will work out for good*, then maybe she could get through the whole ordeal intact. Show the mayor he'd picked the right people. Well, her at least. The jury was still out on Rider.

A few minutes later, she slid into an open parking space in front of Hickory's, the best barbecue restaurant in Bluebonnet—well, probably the whole state of Texas. She checked the parking lot for Rider's monstrosity of a truck but didn't see it. Had she actually beaten him here? She headed inside to wait. The least she could do was get a table.

Jalissa chose a booth for two, but there was still no sign of Rider. After placing their drink order, she shifted her gaze up in time to see him slide onto the bench seat opposite her. He smelled freshly showered, and his damp brown hair curled over his forehead. Seeing him like this, she could admit that Rider held a certain appeal. His ice-blue eyes were captivating and added a charm to his cavalier attitude. The way his brown hair was always perfectly mussed cemented the image she held of him. What would her Mexican grandparents think of her being attracted to a white man?

No, just admitting he has good looks. She definitely was *not* attracted to Rider.

Remembering he wore the Bluebonnet Fire Department blues would be the most effective deterrent to any unwanted feelings and guard her heart from pain. She couldn't trust a guy who joked his way through life—not when it mattered the most—or put himself in danger on a daily basis.

"Thanks for agreeing to come to Hickory's," Rider said. His gaze darted to the menu before lifting back to hers. "Did you order already?"

"Just a drink."

His lips curved in a half smile. "You got a Big Red?"

"Just because we like the same beverage doesn't mean anything." She couldn't forget that time they'd come here with Omar and Trinity. He hadn't been half as annoying as usual.

"I didn't say it did. Is there a small chance you ordered one for me?"

"Yes."

His smile curved into a full-fledged grin. "Appreciate that."

Jalissa rolled her eyes and stared unseeing at the laminated paper before her.

Brenda came over with their sodas and asked if they were ready to order.

"Jalissa?" Rider asked.

"I'll have the barbacoa tacos."

"And you, Rider?"

"I'll have the same."

Jalissa bit back a groan. As soon as Brenda walked out

of hearing, she leaned forward. "Why did you order the same thing?"

"I'm sorry. I didn't see your name next to the tacos on the menu. I was under the impression I could order whatever I wanted."

Jalissa snorted. "Obviously you can, but you mean to tell me that barbacoa is your usual?"

"I order it every time I come." He folded his arms across his chest. "When Poppy's on shift, she doesn't even bother taking my order. Just calls out a welcome and tells me my food will be ready soon. Don't you remember when we came here with Omar and Trinity?"

How had he done it—peeked right inside her brain to the one memory she'd been reflecting on? Instead of answering his questions, she leaned against the backrest, widening the space between them as much as possible. If he wanted to claim barbacoa tacos and Big Red were his favorites—just like hers—she wouldn't argue. *This time.* Even if she talked herself out of commenting, the urge hadn't left.

Why did he get under her skin so much?

Rider leaned forward, placing his elbows on the table. His blue eyes bored into hers, and she resisted the urge to fidget. "So, how are we going to do this, Tucker?"

"I have some ideas." She pointed to her notebook.

"Great." He rubbed his hands together. "I have a few myself." He pulled out a sheet of paper from his back pocket. *Real organized.*

He cocked his head to the side. "Why do you care about the shelter so much?"

She searched his face, looking for any hidden censure, but couldn't find any. "Besides the fact I work there?"

"Yes."

"The animals will most likely die if I don't do something. I couldn't bear that."

"Do you believe animals are more important than humans?" His blue eyes studied hers.

She could feel every nerve ending becoming defensive. "I never said that."

Rider tapped the tabletop with his thumb.

"What?" she groused. "If you have something to say, say it."

"Nah." He shook his head. "I have nothing to say."

"And yet your mouth is still running."

His lips flattened quickly. "I was just trying to gain a little insight. No need to draw the claws."

"Listen, Rider. We're not BFFs or even what I would call friends. We're acquaintances, and the people we know know each other. We're not at the sharing-secrets or baring-private-information level of knowledge. 'Kay?"

He nodded slowly. "Message received loud and clear."

"Good. Now let's get down to business." She took a sip of her Big Red then removed the ribbon holding her place in the notebook.

Rider watched Jalissa as she started writing in her notepad. No frills on it, no bright colors, just a simple navy blue notepad. He pulled his cell out of his back pocket. He'd forgotten a pen or pencil, so his note app would have to work. He switched to his internet browser and did a search for fund-raising ideas in case the few he'd jotted down weren't sufficient for Jalissa.

"I think having a big-ticket item as well as little fund-raising opportunities will be the best," she said.

"That sounds good." He sat back, watching her write in the notebook. What had she come up with?

"Are you even paying attention, Rider?"

Rider shifted his gaze from her delicate hands to the fierce expression darkening her brown eyes. He stifled a sigh. "I'm listening." He pointed to his cell. "Plus, I'm searching for ideas."

"You didn't prepare beforehand?" she sniped.

"Actually, I did. But that doesn't mean I came up with every single solution." He ran a hand through his hair, trying to temper his frustration. The woman could irritate him quicker than a rattler could strike.

She pursed her lips. "All right... I did some research last night, so I understand."

That's big of you. He shook his head inwardly. He needed to rein in the sarcastic thoughts or they'd find their way to his mouth in no time.

"SAFE has a lot of teens who could help us, right?"

"I'm sure some would love to help." Sean being one of them.

"Great. What about having them sell popcorn or chocolate? Those kinds of fund-raisers seem simple enough, don't you think?"

She actually wanted his opinion? *Quit it, Rider. Behave.* "I like that idea. I actually wrote 'selling popcorn.'" He held up the slip of paper he'd taken from Omar on shift earlier. "Or maybe we should do chocolate, like you suggested."

"Well, we have to think about the town and what the people like. Over the years, I've seen fund-raisers for cookie dough, candles, magazines." She threw up her hand. "Maybe if we can gauge people's interest, that might help us narrow it down."

"Or we could sign up for multiple ones?" No need to put all their eggs in one basket. There was a reason that saying existed.

"Yes, we could do that as well." Her brow furrowed as she made notes. "We still need something huge that will bring in the big bucks. I called the mayor, and he said we'd need at least ten thousand for our two programs alone."

Rider gulped. That much? Could their ideas even put a

dent in that? "What about a firefighter calendar?" he suggested. Didn't they always do that in the movies?

Jalissa's eyes widened. "What?"

"Nothing bad or risqué." He tapped his fingers against the tabletop. "You know, maybe we could pair a firefighter with an animal from the shelter. That gives off the sweet vibe. Old women and animal lovers would love it."

"It's actually not a bad idea." She peeked at him as if shocked he had a thought in his brain.

And maybe he shouldn't project. It would only make working with her that more difficult. "Thank you." He paused. "Did that hurt to say?"

She smirked. "Maybe."

He knew it! "The more you practice kindness, the easier it becomes." He couldn't resist poking at her.

Her lips pursed. "For now, let's work on getting these things started. I'll look into what fund-raisers the teens can do and sell around town. You set up the calendar event." Her pen flew across the page. "I'll find out from my boss if there are any prohibitions against using the animals and let you know by the end of the week how many we can use, so you can coordinate the same number of firefighters."

What had he done? Photo shoots? Posing with cats and dogs? The guys at work were going to laugh him out of the station. Him and his big mouth. Still, if it could help Sean and the kids at SAFE, he'd swallow his pride. After he needled hers.

"I assumed we were going with twelve." At her blank expression, he continued. "You know, months in a year. Calendar."

She blinked, then groaned. "Right." She erased something, then wrote again.

Probably making corrections. Jalissa seemed a little too meticulous. "Do you know any good photographers, by any chance?" he asked.

She grinned. "Not a one. Have fun taking care of that." She set her notepad to the side and took a bite of her taco.

Rider wasn't even sure when Brenda had arrived with their orders, but he was glad to have the meal in front of him. He hadn't eaten since end of shift. Silence descended as they turned from talk of money and ate in silence. The quiet was awkward, but as long as he kept his mouth full, he didn't have to worry about what to say.

He could only pray and hope that working with Jalissa wouldn't always be as painful as it was now. After he finished his food, he slid some money into the check holder. "I'll let you know how the planning for the calendar goes and get back to you."

She eyed the bill. "I can pay for my own meal."

"I'm sure you can. *But…* I asked you to meet me here, so I'll pay."

"Rider, I don't want you to take this the wrong way, but I don't want you buying me anything."

Then why did his spine stiffen with offense? "It's not like you'll owe me."

"That's exactly what it'll come down to."

He stared at her. She glared at him.

He huffed and pulled out some of the money. "I'll put enough in here to cover my food and the tip, if that's okay with you, Tucker."

"Perfectly fine, *Rider*. I'll add to the tip, too."

Of course she would. Rider gave her a salute and slid out of the booth. He needed to go by the gym and decompress. Being around her always made him tense and tightly wound. Maybe a few rounds with the punching bag or a good run would tire him out.

Then again, he did need to see if the firefighters would agree to take pictures in their uniforms with rescue animals. Did he have to get that approved with HR? He rubbed his chin as he walked to his truck and tried to shove his meeting with Jalissa out of his mind.

Yet he could still see that stubborn tilt of her chin. The irritation that flashed in her eyes when he tried to pay for their meal. Being around her would have him exercising every fruit of the spirit. But he had a feeling he would continue to come up short and keep praying for forgiveness.

Chapter Four

Rover dashed forward, ears flopping in the wind as his paws covered the fenced yard. He picked up the tennis ball Jalissa had thrown and ran back to her.

"Good boy, Rover." She rubbed his head, taking the slobbery toy from his mouth before chucking it in the air again.

Rover wouldn't have been her first pick of a name, but somehow the moniker suited the Old English sheepdog. After his owner had passed away unexpectedly, the owner's adult children hadn't wanted the upkeep of a pet, so to the shelter he'd gone.

Jalissa prayed he'd be adopted soon. She'd placed him on every pet-finder board she could think of. Since he was already potty trained and knew basic commands, he'd make a great companion. More than a pet, he'd been someone's family and didn't deserve to be discarded like the unwanted sofa at a garage sale.

The thought had her wheels spinning. Maybe she and Rider could do some kind of adoption event. Technically, a function like that didn't fall under fund-raising, but if her idea got the animals rehomed, she'd consider it a win. Plus, the shelter's expenses would decrease with fewer mouths to feed.

She pulled out her cell phone and noted the idea. Before she changed her mind, she texted Rider.

Jalissa: What if we have an adoption event at the shelter? Not exactly a fund-raiser, but could defray overall costs.

Baneofmyexistence: If you request donations, we'd still raise money.

Jalissa: We already charge for adoptions.

Baneofmyexistence: Nothing says you can't ask for more help.

She bit her lip. Was he insinuating something? Jalissa blew out a breath and pushed the thought out of her mind. She was in a good head space and didn't need Rider to spin her around.

Baneofmyexistence: Can you come by the firehouse around five and discuss the photo shoot?

Never! She avoided that place as if obeying a restraining order. No use risking outrage and remembering the heartache of her father's death.

Jalissa: I'll pass.

Baneofmyexistence: I don't get off until Friday, though. We need to know what kind of background we want for the calendar. Did you find out about use of animals?

Jalissa: Won't the photographer have backgrounds?

Baneofmyexistence: Oh. Right.

Jalissa: I'll have an answer about the animals by end of day.

She shook her head and called for Rover. His time in the yard was over, and she needed to bring out the puppies. A local farmer had discovered them in a box at the edge of his property. The mixed-breed pups were about fifteen weeks old, and the vet had guessed them to have boxer and mastiff ancestry. They were going to be huge, judging by their paws.

Many of her volunteers begged to exercise them, and she understood because taking them out brought her joy. So, she assigned people turns to cuddle with the pups.

Jalissa led Rover to his outdoor pen. The weather was a perfect seventy degrees today, and all the dogs were enjoying some sunshine. September in Texas didn't always have such mild temps.

She washed her hands, then headed for the puppy pen to grab the five cuties. Their droopy snouts were adorable and melted her heart. She and Quinn had named them after famous boxers. There were two girls, Ali and Sugar, and the boys were Tyson, Floyd and Manny.

"Oh, are you getting the puppies?" Kylie asked. "Can I help?"

Jalissa peered up at the high school volunteer from her crouched position. As a senior, Kylie didn't have a last period of the day. Instead, she spent her time volunteering at the shelter, since she had aspirations of becoming a veterinarian.

"Sure. Could you grab the leashes?"

"Coming right up." The teen smiled, her black ponytail bouncing with movement as she headed for the leash cabinet.

Jalissa unlatched the pen, letting the dogs climb all over her. Kylie handed her leash after leash as Jalissa slipped the straps around their necks. Some of the pups hated being led around, but Jalissa had high hopes the puppies would be adopted soon, so they would need to get used to it. They walked the pups to the fenced-in yard and let them loose. She and Kylie began chatting as the puppies tromped around the grass, stretching out their gangly legs.

"Do you think the mayor will really close the shelter?" Kylie asked softly.

"I hope not." Jalissa threw a couple of balls and watched the pups scramble after the toys. "It would be a shame. I know we don't have adoptions daily, but we do rehome a lot of the pets."

"I'll help. I'll do whatever you need me to do, Ms. Jalissa."

"Thank you." She rubbed her forehead. "I talked to a fund-raising company, and we're going to sell citronella candles, jerky and popcorn. Rider said he'd ask the teens at SAFE to help out."

"Well, put me down on the list, too. I can ask my friends at school if they want to help as well."

"Thank you." She offered a smile to Kylie. Knowing she could add at least one person to the list made Jalissa relax a bit. Hopefully Rider would have an easy time of getting the firefighters to pose for the calendar.

She was thankful he'd thought of the idea and she could pawn the work off on him. No way did she want to step foot in that place and remember. She sniffed and crouched down, rubbing Ali's soft fur.

Ever since the mayor's announcement, Jalissa had walked around with a weight on her chest. The tightness didn't ease and had her tossing and turning every night. If their efforts didn't start showing results, her tenuous hold on normality would slip between her fingers.

"You want me to do what?" Omar Young's mouth curled in disgust like he'd just stepped on a stink bug and smelled the repercussions.

"Jalissa and I were tasked with raising money for some of Bluebonnet's programs that depend on town funding. She wants the animal shelter to stay open, and I'm pulling for SAFE."

"And you think having me pose with a dog for a calendar is going to raise enough money to save those outreaches?"

Hearing the question voiced out loud brought heat to Rider's neck. Omar was a good friend, but if he was having this reaction, what would the other guys say? "Maybe not *all* the money we need, but come on—" Rider threw his hands in the air "—women love firefighters and pets. Put them both together, and we're sure to sell tons of calendars."

Omar rubbed his chin. "I don't know, man. I'm not sure how Trinity would feel about me posing for a calendar."

Rider scoffed. "I'm not asking you to do anything indecent. Hold the dog while wearing your uniform and smile for the camera. Easy."

"Has anyone else said yes?"

Rider paused. "So, you see—"

"I knew it," Omar interjected.

"But if you say yes, the other guys are bound to agree, too." God willing. Rider just needed twelve of them to say yes. Well, eleven. He couldn't ask them without agreeing to do it himself.

"Just hold a dog and smile for the camera?" Omar asked cautiously.

"Exactly. No sweat."

Omar huffed. "Fine, man. I'll do it."

Rider leaned against the locker in the bay area. "Thanks, man. I appreciate that."

"No problem. I'm sure Trinity will be helping Jalissa in some way, too."

"Good. The more help we can get from the community, the better."

Omar cocked his head to the side. "Watch it. You're starting to sound like a grown-up."

"Yeah, well, chasing down thirty kind of does that to you."

"I don't know. It's like you've settled down. You're

volunteering at SAFE, doing this fund-raiser…" Omar shrugged. "Good on you, man."

Rider nodded, but inside he might have felt a tad warm and embarrassed by the kind words. When he'd first started working at the station, Omar had made it obvious that Rider annoyed him. But Rider hadn't let that deter him from turning Omar into a friend. Now Omar handled Rider's jokes good-naturedly. He didn't know if that meant he'd matured or if their friendship came with a certain level of understanding.

Rider clapped Omar on the back. "Thanks again. I'm going to go ask the other guys on shift."

"You got this." Omar smirked.

"I hope so."

A few of the guys turned him down flat, not even letting him explain how it could help the town. They shook their heads and walked away. Rider slid his hands into his uniform pockets.

He got it—posing for a calendar while holding a pet threatened some guys' masculinity, or maybe they didn't want to be on display for whatever reason. But Rider had hoped the appeal of community spirit would keep the guys from dismissing him outright. He pulled out a bar stool at the kitchen island and rested his head in his hands.

"Who killed your dog, Rider?" Captain Simms asked.

Rider straightened, eyeing the captain as the man grabbed a bottled water from the fridge. "No one, sir. I don't own a dog."

"Then why do you look like the milk expired and you have nothing to put in your cereal?"

"I need volunteers, and the men aren't feeling too charitable."

Captain Simms's thin eyebrows rose. The older man had chosen to shave his head completely bald. The look had Rider constantly guessing Simms's age.

"Volunteers for what?"

The captain's no-nonsense tone had Rider detailing the plans for the calendar and the causes they were trying to support.

"Hmm. You only need twelve men, right?"

"Yes, sir. Well, ten now. Omar agreed to help, and of course, I'll be a man of the month as well." His face heated. That sounded ridiculous.

"Smart of you." Captain Simms poured himself a cup of coffee, then peered at Rider over the rim. "Count me in as well."

"Really?" Rider leaned forward, wondering just what the captain would require of him to seal the deal. Captain Simms was a little tougher on Rider than the others. He didn't know if that was because he'd transferred from Dallas or what. Though Rider had attended high school in Bluebonnet, he'd left once he had diploma in hand. But city life hadn't appealed, so Uncle Jay had helped secure Rider a job here, and the rest had been history.

"I will. I'll even make an announcement letting the men know they should all sign up."

"Wow, Cap, that's awesome." Rider cleared his throat, his thumb tapping out a nervous rhythm. "Uh, is there anything I should do in return?"

Captain Simms's lips quirked. "I'm good, son. Just want to help out."

Huh. "Then thank you."

"Do you have a photographer yet?"

"No, sir." He needed to add that to his to-do list.

"My wife is a good photographer."

Rider hid a smile. "Oh, yeah? Does she have a website I can contact her through?"

Captain Simms pulled a business card from his pocket and slid it across the island countertop. "Sure does."

Rider chuckled. There it was. But having the captain's

wife do the photo shoot was a quid pro quo Rider could handle. "I'll call her, sir."

"She'll appreciate the business."

That evening Rider took a spot at the firehouse dining table with the rest of the fellas. Captain Simms said grace, then after a chorus of amens they started passing the serving platters around. Captain Simms cleared his throat.

"Listen up. Y'all've probably heard that Rider is coordinating fund-raising efforts with Jalissa Tucker. They're going to do a photo shoot to sell calendars, and Rider needs y'all to step up to the plate." Captain Simms caught his gaze. "How many have said yes?"

"Three, sir. Counting myself, I have four total." He'd convinced Trent to say yes while he pumped iron.

"Philips, how many months in a year?" barked Captain Simms.

"Twelve, sir."

"How many more men does Rider need to help out, Carter?"

Carter choked on a spoonful of mac and cheese. He wiped his uniform. "Eight, sir."

"How many of y'all can help Rider?"

Every man who hadn't volunteered shot his hand up in the air. Counting the captain and himself, his tally added to seven. Not bad. Rider nodded and gave them all his thanks.

"I'll be sure to hit up the other shift so you can get your twelve."

"Appreciate that, Cap." Rider stared down at his plate so he wouldn't let out the laughter building within him.

If he'd known the captain would be on his side from the get-go, Rider would have started there and saved himself the embarrassment of asking each man on shift. He pulled out his cell and opened up his messages with Jalissa.

Rider: I've got the men—well, once the other shift agrees. Got the photographer—as soon as I email her. Now we need a place to do the photo shoot.

Miss 'tude: That's great! It's really coming together. What about the field near the church?

Bluebonnet Community Church sat on a couple of acres. Too bad it wasn't spring, or they could have had bluebonnets in the picture. Still, having that white steeple in the background might make a perfectly wholesome backdrop and drive up sales.

Rider: That could work.

Miss 'tude: Don't jump for joy and excitement.

He shook his head.

Rider: It's not a bad idea. I simply like more than one option.

Miss 'tude: Well it's your fund-raiser idea, so get to brainstorming.

He snorted. Even in text she had attitude for days.

Rider: Will do. Meet up tomorrow? We can go over everything we've set up.

Miss 'tude: I'm supposed to go over to Trinity's for dinner. I'll see if she has food for one more.

Rider: Don't bother her. I can meet you afterward.

Miss 'tude: Too late. She says come on over.

Rider: Then I'll see you tomorrow.

Miss 'tude: I can't wait.

Rider: Don't roll your eyes and inject sarcasm across the screen. I know it's a front.

Jalissa sent an *as if* GIF. He chuckled and slid his cell back into his pocket.

"Looking awfully chipper over there," Omar murmured, taking a bite of his food.

"Just enjoy joking around."

"Ha! Don't I know it."

What could he say? Interjecting humor into tense moments had been a way to escape some of the bullying situations he'd found himself in as a teen. He'd been one of the few kids who didn't have a dad and had coped with food. He'd heard every fat joke known to man growing up, but he'd discovered if he joked back, a lot of his tormentors would leave him alone. His uncle had told him confidence could be a deterrent in certain situations, so Rider had become *slightly* overconfident. Not that he'd call himself arrogant or anything. He simply knew how to portray an image the public wanted. Even when he didn't feel the truth of the persona.

If people thought that made him vain, then so be it. He didn't owe anyone but his maker an explanation for how he got through the trials of life.

Chapter Five

The coolness of Jalissa's iced sweet tea took an edge off the high temps that had surprised everyone today. Though the calendar said September, today's gauge still pointed toward summer highs. Jalissa placed the glass on the bistro table next to her rocking chair. Nothing like relaxing on the front porch and hanging out with your two best friends. She rubbed Flo's head.

"You're awfully quiet today," Trinity remarked.

"Enjoying your company." And wondering what dinner with Rider would be like. Would he make the evening difficult?

Trinity laughed. "Or you're worried about Rider coming over."

Jalissa's cheeks heated. "We've been in each other's presence before without any bloodshed." Once or twice.

"You can't see internal bleeding."

Jalissa's lips quirked, but she told herself it was a reaction to the antics of Faith and Joy, who were taking turns pushing each other on the tire swing in front of the Youngs' home, not Trinity's quip.

"Rider's darts don't draw blood. They just make me angry."

"They're supposed to make you laugh." Exasperation coated Trinity's words.

"He's not as funny as he thinks he is." Why couldn't he be serious? People had hard things they were going through without someone coming around and making a joke of everything. She prayed he had enough sense to put the humor aside when the fire alarm sounded. People in crisis situations needed firefighters dedicated to their jobs, willing to lay down their lives and ensure those in danger kept theirs, if it came to that.

She blinked back tears. Flo nudged her hand, prompting Jalissa to continue the affections and allow her heart rate to return to normal.

"What's going on in your brain, girl? It doesn't seem like a peaceful quiet over there," Trinity said from her rocking chair.

"I don't understand why Rider has to joke about everything. Would it hurt him to be a little more serious?" Jalissa took a sip of her drink. "Maybe it's because he's so young."

"He's not *that* young," Trinity shot back.

"He's gotta be, what…twenty-five?" she asked.

"Uh, no. Rider's thirty or turning thirty soon."

Huh. Who knew he was only two years younger than her? She'd never date anyone younger than her. Not that she'd ever date Rider.

You don't date firefighters, remember?

How could she forget? Yet for a brief moment, her mind had cataloged Rider's attributes—employed, good-looking, loyal—and rated him on a possible eligible-bachelor scale. His status as a firefighter, plus his annoying arrogance, constant jokes and being two years younger simply tallied up the cons column. Not that she was tallying anything.

"Still too young," Jalissa said.

"Two years is nothing."

"I prefer older men." Though if she didn't date, was that really a preference or an idea?

Trinity chuckled. "Well I'm sure you're not thinking of dating Rider anytime soon, are you?"

Jalissa's jaw dropped. "Of course not." She faked a shudder and earned a look of annoyance from Flo as the dog's chin got jostled in the process. "I'm just saying he could stand to be a little more serious now and then. I'm sure there's a man out there who's a happy medium. Great age and knows how to have fun."

"I'm sure you'll find whomever you're looking for."

Did she really want to? All her close friends were either married or divorced and starting another relationship already. Here she sat, never been married and unattached. Self-preservation at its finest. Was that a good thing? "Is there something wrong with me?"

"No." Trinity reached over and squeezed her arm. "What is going on with you? Are you sure you're okay?"

"Guess I'm just taking stock of my life." Jalissa shrugged. "I'm not in a relationship, not married, I'm just…" She sighed.

"A wonderful woman who works with animals, is raising funds to help local programs, my best friend and a child of God. Sure, I could add other labels if you want me to continue. But know this—not being in a romantic relationship doesn't negate your worth. Not everyone is called to marriage anyway."

Though the words affirmed her, Jalissa still couldn't shake that unsettling feeling tossing her stomach to and fro. Sometimes she got lonely. Sure, Flo was an excellent companion and helped Jalissa process anxiety and other worries. But at the end of the day, she still came home to an empty house.

But that frees you from the pain of disappointment and widowhood.

The front door opened, and Omar stepped out. "Steaks are ready." He glanced at the driveway in front of their white farmhouse. "No sign of Rider yet?"

"Not yet." Trinity smiled up at Omar, and he leaned down to kiss her forehead.

Jalissa turned away, allowing her friend to have a private moment. When Trinity had first told Jalissa she'd married Omar for convenience, Jalissa had been rocked to the core. Their marriage had seemed like settling to her, not to mention the danger of marrying a firefighter. Yet witnessing them fall in love had softened her to their union. Some days, her heart ached watching them together. Not that she could ever marry for convenience. Still, it was tempting to jump into a relationship in order to call someone her own.

What is wrong with you? Shake the melancholy.

A grumble filled the air, and Rider's truck rumbled up the street. He was the perfect person for her to focus on. She could list all his faults and remind herself why dating wasn't a good idea. She had to remember that God had good plans for her. Surely, Jeremy Rider was in no way a part of them.

He jumped out of his truck and sauntered up the sidewalk before climbing the porch steps. "Evening, folks."

"Glad you made it, man." Omar pulled Rider in for a back clap.

"Evening, Trinity… Jalissa." His gaze stopped on hers.

She swallowed. "Rider." See? She could be cordial.

"I just told the ladies the steaks are ready. You hungry?" Omar asked.

"I brought my appetite." Rider patted his flat stomach.

"Great. Let's go inside." Omar cupped his mouth. "Faith! Joy! Dinner!"

The girls shrieked and jumped off the swing, running all the way up the porch. Trinity took them inside to wash their hands, and Jalissa followed behind them. Soon they all sat at the picnic table in the backyard. Citronella candles burned around the back deck, keeping the bugs at bay.

Jalissa pointed out the yellow wax–filled jars. "Those are one of our fund-raising ideas."

"The candles?" Trinity asked, brow furrowing.

"Mmm-hmm. No one likes bugs, so I figured people would buy them."

"Smart," Omar said.

"Let's save the fund-raiser talk until after dinner or dessert time," Rider suggested.

She straightened in her chair. "Is there a problem with talking about it now?"

"No," he responded cautiously. "I just thought you might need a break from all things fund-raiser."

She nodded, taking a bite to prevent her from further elevating the situation. Too bad her body had already activated the fight-or-flight system. Her nerves strummed tight, ready to pounce on any derisive comment from Rider's lips.

Jalissa kept quiet as the conversation moved from topic to topic. Trinity shot her worried glances, forcing Jalissa to have a ready smile on her lips each time. Her hopes of reassuring her friend fell flat when Trinity asked Jalissa to help gather the dishes. Flo followed, never letting Jalissa out of sight. As soon as they were inside, Trinity started questioning her.

"Is your anxiety up?" Trinity asked softly. "Is that why you brought Flo?"

"No, actually, I feel good today. Flo and I had a nice run around the neighborhood this morning." She hadn't needed to count at all today. "I just wanted her company just in case." In the event Rider had her needing to count and loosen the band around her chest.

"You haven't made one crack at Rider."

Jalissa raised an eyebrow. "You always tell me to behave."

"True." Trinity laughed. "I suppose I've never seen you so contemplative."

"I have my moments." Jalissa gently bumped Trinity's hip. "I'll grab everyone more drinks and you'll get the dessert?"

"Okay, but promise me something."

Jalissa paused, two bottled sodas in hand. "Sure, Trin."

"If you ever need to talk, you'll call me?"

"All right," she whispered, but Jalissa doubted she ever would. Experience had taught her she was stronger on her own. She didn't need to share her problems or lean on another person.

"Wow, Trinity, this cake is life," Rider pronounced after taking a bite. He sectioned off another piece and then scooped up a bit of ice cream, too.

"I made it with Big Red."

"She's amazing," Omar said.

"So good." Jalissa did a happy dance as she followed one bite with another.

Rider couldn't help but think how adorable she was when happy. "I take it this is Jalissa's favorite." He gestured toward her with his fork.

Trinity laughed. "You know it."

Rider eyed his food, a thought occurring to him. "Is the cake sugar-free?"

Trinity was a Type 1 diabetic, and Rider would never forget that day the fire department responded to a call at the Young household last year. Omar had been beside himself with worry as they sped from the station. Rider thought the incident was probably what tipped Young to finally admit he was falling in love with his wife. Not that they talked about things like that. Merely speculation on Rider's part.

"No. I decided to skip dessert today. This little tyke—" Trinity patted her stomach "—is happiest when I fuel up on protein."

Explained why she was eating another steak. "Growing a Texas boy, huh?"

Omar and Trinity shared a secret glance. The kind that came with a close marriage—or so Rider assumed. He didn't actually know, considering his father had left his mom before he was even born. It was why his last name was her maiden one. And though he'd lived near Uncle Jay and Aunt Mara for a few years, it wasn't the same as coming from a two-parent household. As cool as those secret glances were, Rider didn't want to enter a relationship to have one. Couldn't risk that he'd have one more person walk away without a backward glance.

Trinity broke the silence. "We just found out we're having a boy."

"Congrats!" Jalissa cried, getting up to hug Trinity.

"That's amazing. Congratulations, guys." Rider smiled at the happy couple.

"I thought you didn't want to know," Jalissa said.

"Doctor accident." Trinity and Omar shared another glance. "But we're both happy."

Rider was glad they weren't the type of couple to set their friends up in the name of "happiness" or "romance." He'd dated enough women to know that most didn't have staying power. They either were too superficial and were interested in him because of the uniform or couldn't hang with his lifestyle. He liked a life of adventure. Not anything to cross the line of legality, but maybe jumping out of a plane to experience the glory of free falling, or hitting a white-water rapid trail. So far, most of his dates couldn't even handle a simple hike.

His gaze darted to Jalissa. She had a lean figure that made him wonder if she was the outdoorsy type. In a different world, he would have asked her out. Not because he thought they would have a lasting relationship, but because there were only so many people in Bluebonnet to date. He was always up front that he just wanted someone to hang with.

As it was, he couldn't survive Jalissa's presence for ten minutes without having to pray to God for patience. The idea of a date had sailed away with all the fanfare of a bon voyage. Her constant prickly nature had overshadowed the allure of her pretty smile and loyalty to her best friend.

"We're so excited," Trinity said.

"You going to name him Junior?" Rider asked.

Omar smiled down at his wife. "We're still discussing names."

"Rider makes a good first name." He shrugged. "Just saying."

"Tucker makes a good first name." Jalissa wrinkled her nose. "Never mind."

They all laughed.

"Rider, I heard that Captain Simms's wife is doing the photo shoot. Is that right?" Trinity asked.

"She is. Jalissa suggested we take the pictures with the chapel as the background."

"Oh, I like that idea," Trinity said.

Omar shook his head.

"What?" Jalissa said, hand on hip.

"It's firefighters and dogs. It should be at the firehouse, or at least have an engine in the background."

"Mmm. Good point." Rider took out his cell to make a note. "Do you have any other ideas?"

"You want us to do all your work for ya?" Omar joked.

"I consider it outsourcing."

"You would," Jalissa said.

Despite the heat that rose up his neck, Rider ignored the dig. Sooner or later, he'd need to have a little chat with his fund-raising cochair. But not when they were with friends.

"You need an item that will bring in the big bucks," Trinity suggested.

"That's what I said," Jalissa exclaimed.

"How big?" Omar asked. "Are you talking renting a projector screen and showing movies for a cheaper price? Wait, is that even legal?"

"Good question," Jalissa said.

It was a good idea, but a quick internet search on his cell told Rider it wouldn't work. He shared the info with his friends.

"Bummer," Trinity said.

Rider snapped his fingers. "What about a coupon book people can purchase? The coupons will be from local businesses. Gives them incentive to see us succeed."

"Wow, Rider, that's not a bad plan." Jalissa gave a slow nod.

"I have a good idea or two."

She smirked.

"Hey, Jalissa, can you hook me up with a docile dog for the photo shoot?" Omar asked.

She nodded. "Sure can. My supervisor okayed the use of the animals. She only asked that the shelter be mentioned so people know where to go if they get that adoption bug." She rubbed her hands together. "I also have some adorable puppies that would be perfect for the shoot."

"Are they potty trained?"

Rider threw his head back, laughing at the uneasy expression on Omar's face. He caught his breath. "If our uniforms can take the heat…"

"Heat and bodily fluids are two different things, man. That's probably a stain I can't get out in the wash."

"Can't be worse than the skunk incident," Trinity said with a grin.

Rider's shoulders shook as he tried to suppress his laughter. He'd never forget when Omar had gotten skunked on a call. They'd all worn their masks back to the firehouse so they wouldn't have to breathe in the noxious fumes.

Omar shook his head, but an amused grin filled his face. "Anybody want more cake?"

"Oh, wait up, babe. I need to bring in these dishes." Trinity reached for his dessert plate.

Rider stood. "Let me help."

"No. You two talk fund-raising stuff."

He sat back down in time to see Jalissa pull out her little notebook. Where had she hidden that?

"Captain Simms's wife is doing the shoot, then? Did she say when?"

"She'd like to do it next weekend," Rider said. "I happen to be off then, too, so I thought it was a good day."

"Great. Did she have any location suggestions?"

"Besides the chapel?"

Jalissa nodded.

"No, but she did say she'd email me tomorrow. I like Omar's suggestion of the firehouse, so I'll email her that one."

Jalissa's eyes grew wide as she met his stare. "I'm not sure that's a good idea."

"Why not?" Did her dislike extend to all things fire-fighting related?

"I don't really go there."

He arched an eyebrow. "Care to explain?" Because now his curiosity was piqued.

"Not really."

He tapped the table. "If we end up choosing that location, is that going to be a problem?"

She worried her bottom lip. When her dog nudged her, Jalissa's shoulders relaxed, then she finally shook her head.

Rider let out the air he'd been holding hostage. "And the fund-raisers for the kids? How's that going?"

"I received your list of names, added the ones I had and contacted everyone. I've got half of them enrolled." She slid a piece of paper across the table. "These are the SAFE kids I couldn't reach. Could you have them call me?"

"Sure thing." He scanned the list. Sean was on there. "Sean's mom doesn't answer unknown numbers. I'll be sure to tell her to call you back."

"I think that was one of the numbers I couldn't leave a message on."

He nodded. "No worries. I'll get him squared away."

She studied him. "Do you know him personally?"

"He's my pal. I mentor him."

Something flashed in her eyes. "How long have you been doing that?"

"A year. It was difficult in the beginning, but now we're friends."

"It's pretty nice of you to volunteer your time that way."

She sounded impressed. Rider wanted to tell her he had a brain and a heart. It was obvious that she didn't think that much of him, but he didn't have the energy to get into it right now.

He cleared his throat. "I wouldn't be who I was if I hadn't been mentored. Every young man needs a good male role model."

"It's nice you had your dad to guide you through life." A rueful expression twisted her lips.

"I didn't." He stood, ignoring her and praying she didn't have a look of pity on her face. "I'll text you the photo shoot time and dates. See ya."

Rider hauled himself inside, said his goodbyes to Omar and Trinity, then headed home as if he'd entered a timed physical fitness exam. He wanted to escape the memories and all the times he'd wondered why he hadn't been good enough for his dad to stick around. Why he hadn't been good enough for the teens at school to offer him friendship instead of making his life miserable. And maybe he should remind himself that Jalissa had been part of that crowd as well.

Chapter Six

"Mija, tie those with a green ribbon." Mamí pointed to the tamales piling up before her.

"Sí, Mamí." Jalissa resisted the urge to wipe her forehead. Her hair had been gathered into a ponytail, and she'd donned a tank top and shorts to keep from overheating in Mamí's kitchen.

They were supposed to meet up with her father's side of the family today for a picnic. Which was why Jalissa had come over bright and early to help assemble the tamales, her mother's signature dish for potlucks of all kinds. Mamí had made chicken, beef and pork carnitas, and now Jalissa had to tie a piece of string on each end, using a different color to differentiate between the three meat choices.

It's way too early for this.

She blinked slowly as her mind struggled to wake up.

"Mija, here." Mamí waved a mug in front of Jalissa's face, the tantalizing scent of coffee like a jolt of adrenaline to her system.

"Mmm." Jalissa tied the last ribbon and took the drink. "Gracias."

"De nada. I can't have you falling asleep. We still have dessert to make."

Jalissa groaned. "More cooking?"

Mamí arched an eyebrow. "¿Cómo? Did I miss you standing over the stove creating a masterpiece in this kitchen?"

"Sorry," Jalissa mumbled. But seriously, it was too early for this.

"Don't be. You can get started on the empanadas. I figured we'd make fruit ones."

"Which kind?"

"Pineapple and apple." Mamí pointed to the ingredients laid out on the island.

Jalissa's nose wrinkled as she stared at the fixings. On a sigh, she rolled up her sleeves. "I'll get started."

"Thank you, my daughter." Jalissa preferred the Spanish version, mija. In English, her mother's comment sounded like a chastisement.

For the next few hours, they chatted while readying the food. The empanadas came out a golden brown when Jalissa pulled them from the oven. She placed a prepared sheet pan of uncooked ones in the heated range, then turned to place the hot pastries on the cooling rack. After this last batch, they would head to the park where the Tucker family would gather for an impromptu reunion.

Granted, it wasn't a *true* family reunion. It would only be her grandparents, a couple of aunts and uncles, and maybe some cousins. Still, being around the Tuckers always brightened Jalissa's day and made her feel less alone in the world.

Not that I am alone, Lord. I know You're always with me. I just can't always tell. She had no idea if that was a mark against her faith or her sense of awareness. Either way, she didn't like not being able to feel the connection at will.

Jalissa shook the thoughts from her mind and turned to the task at hand. She packaged the empanadas while her mother took care of the tamales. Soon they had the trunk loaded with goodies. Jalissa buckled Flo in the back seat with her car safety harness before sliding into the front passenger seat.

Half an hour later, Mamí drove over the speed bump leading into the park. The Tuckers had chosen the county park because it held more picnic areas than the one in Bluebonnet. Though they lived a few hours away, they were always willing to cover the distance if it meant seeing Jalissa and Mamí.

After unlatching Flo and letting her out, Jalissa grabbed the container of empanadas and headed toward the picnic shelter. She could see Gran seated under an umbrella, her feet up on a fold-out chaise.

"Jalissa, baby," Gran called out, a smile covering her wrinkled face.

Gran was really her great-grandmother, but everyone called her Gran. Jalissa bent down and kissed her cheek as the older woman wrapped her arms around Jalissa's neck. "My precious baby girl. How are you, huh?" She cupped Jalissa's face in her wizened hands.

"Tired, Gran. Mamí had me cooking early today."

"That's why you prep the day before. All you gotta do then is slip it in the oven."

"I worked late, Gran." Mamí bent and kissed both of Gran's cheeks then placed her offerings on the rectangular table. "Besides, cooking this morning gave me time to hang out with this beauty." Mamí wrapped an arm around Jalissa's shoulders.

Whenever they visited the Tuckers, Jalissa's mother always became more demonstrative. She didn't know why, but she'd learned to expect the small touches.

"Where's my grandpup?" Gran asked.

Jalissa whistled, and Flo came running to her side. She ran her fingers through the dog's soft fur. "She likes to explore new places."

Gran placed her feet on the ground and motioned for Flo to come. She rubbed behind Flo's ears, making cooing noises. Flo leaned her head back, one back leg starting to twitch from enjoyment. Jalissa chuckled and turned away.

Soon the rest of the family showed up. Uncle David and his wife gave Jalissa hugs and began chatting up her mom. Jalissa took the opportunity to sneak away and get a little peace and quiet. As much as she loved her extended family, they could be a little rowdy. Since she'd grown up an only child, that much noise overwhelmed her if she didn't take a break. She headed for one of the trails, Flo falling right into step.

Jalissa inhaled deeply, noting the scents in the air. That faint hint of barbecue Grandpa had grilling in the park's pit. Though the smell of charcoal lingered in the air, with every step away from the shelter, the scent faded. Just as her mind sighed in relief at the newly discovered quiet, a new sound reached her ears. Footsteps rustled along the dirt path. Someone else was on the trail.

She immediately moved to the right, and Flo tromped through the grass. Jalissa tensed as one of the voices became distinctly familiar. *No, Lord. What are the odds?* She slowed her steps, but it was no use. As she rounded the bend, Rider came into view. Actually, Rider and a teen— most likely his SAFE pal.

Jalissa waved, then slid her hand into her shorts pocket, feeling foolish. Rider blinked in surprise while the teen looked back and forth between them.

"Hi," she said. Better get the awkward over with.

"Hey," Rider said. "What are you doing way out here?"

She pointed a thumb over her shoulder. "Picnic with the fam. You?"

"Hiking with the bud." He laid a hand on the young man's shoulder. "This is Sean. Sean, this is Jalissa."

Sean stuck out a hand. "Nice to meet you, ma'am."

She forced her face not to show the surprise at his excellent manners. Then again, his mom had probably taught Sean, not the man beside him. "Nice to meet you, too." She returned the handshake, then shifted on her feet, reaching for Flo.

"Oh, don't go that way." Rider pointed over his shoulder, blocking the path. "They must have gotten rain in the area yesterday. It's nothing but mud up ahead."

"Oh. Uh, thanks." Great. How could she escape this awkwardness then?

"Sure."

Somehow, they all fell in line as they headed back down the trail toward the picnic area. The silence clawed at her, and she wracked her brain for a topic. "How long have you been here?"

"Maybe ten minutes?" Rider responded. "Sean and I are gonna throw the disc around before he has to get back home."

Jalissa peeked at the teen in question. He had a casual smile on his face, like he wanted to keep his cool.

"Can I pet your dog?" Sean asked.

Jalissa made a motion for Flo to stop. "Sure. Just introduce yourself to her. She doesn't like sudden movements or strangers." But since she wasn't wearing her vest, Flo would be more open to the introduction.

Sean knelt down and held out his hand. "I'm Sean."

"This is Flo," Jalissa said.

"Strange name for a dog."

Rider laughed. "Probably after the famous runner, Flo-Jo, right?"

Jalissa nodded, too surprised Rider had caught the reference. Whatever Sean said to her dog worked—Flo bent her head and Sean stroked her fur softly.

"She's so soft."

"That's one of my favorite things about her." Nothing relaxed her more than petting her companion.

"Jalissa!" A shout rose from ahead. Sounded like Uncle David.

"Go, Flo." Hopefully they'd see the dog and assume she was right behind. "I've got to go. See ya around."

Rider gave her a brief nod in understanding, and Jalissa

hurried down the trail. She stopped abruptly to keep from running into her cousin.

"Yikes." She placed a hand on her heart. "You scared me, Mark."

He grinned. "Did I interrupt something here?" He motioned behind her.

Jalissa turned and spotted Rider and Sean. "Oh, just ran into some…friends."

"Oh, cool." He introduced himself, offering a hand to Rider and Sean. "Any friend of Jalissa's is a friend of the Tucker family. Y'all want to join us for some food?"

Sean's eyes got all big, and a sinking feeling filled Jalissa's stomach. She didn't want to introduce Rider to her family. What if they got the wrong idea?

"I think they're about to play a game, Mark."

Sean's face fell, and her heart dropped right to her toes. She couldn't hurt the young man just to spite Rider. "But, uh, if Rider doesn't mind delaying the game…"

Sean whirled around to face the man in question. "Do you mind?"

"Not at all, kiddo. If you want to join them, and they're cool with it, then sure." Rider shrugged.

"Great, man," Mark said. "Just follow us. There's plenty of food."

Yeah, great.

Rider could tell by the frozen expression on Jalissa's face that she was far from happy that he and Sean had intruded upon her family's picnic. He reached for her arm to stay her. Instead, she yanked away from him and turned, a glare piercing him through and through. He held up his hands.

"I meant no harm." He swallowed. "Just wanted to make sure you're okay with us joining you." He pointed at her cousin's retreating back, thankful Sean had followed behind him. "Sean and I don't have to eat with y'all. We'll be fine on our own."

That was their status quo. He didn't even hang out with Sean's mom. Sometimes they played games with the others at SAFE, but Sean preferred one-on-one interactions. *Most of the time.*

Jalissa folded her arms. "Sorry, I didn't mean to give you the stink eye." She sighed. "It's fine. Like Mark said, we have plenty of food."

"You're sure?" Because irritation seemed to be coming off her in waves. Whether that was just the welcome he got or something else, he couldn't tell.

"Ask me again, Rider."

He stifled a chuckle at her demand. Seriously, why did he enjoy riling her up? Maybe he could sweeten the pot. "Thank you for your hospitality."

She rolled her eyes and stalked forward.

Or maybe not. The desire to grin beckoned, but he'd maintain his cool. Maybe he should dial it down and show Sean good manners. He didn't feel like explaining the dynamic that was his relationship with Jalissa. Not that they were in a relationship—more of a...workship? Was that a thing?

He shrugged. It was now. When he caught up to the young man and Jalissa's cousin, Sean tugged on his arm.

"What's up, bud?"

"That's not how I pictured Jalissa," Sean whispered.

Rider raised an eyebrow. "How did you picture her?"

"Taller," Sean stated simply.

Rider laughed. "When she's mad, it's like she gains height." Sean eyed him skeptically, so Rider nodded. "It's true, man."

They soon reached the picnic tables. Her family had commandeered one under a shaded veranda. Rider thanked the Lord for small blessings, because it was another hot September day.

An older woman stood, and Jalissa motioned for Rider to follow. He swallowed, mouth suddenly as dry as air during a Texas bushfire.

"Rider, this is my gran. Gran, this is my friend Rider and his friend Sean."

Rider extended his hand. "Nice to meet you, ma'am."

"Pleasure's all mine." Her rheumy eyes lit with delight, and she widened her arms to fold him into the warmest hug he'd had in a long time. He closed his eyes, holding her lightly in his arms. She smelled like apple pie. If his grandmother had lived, would she exude love like this?

He pulled back, suddenly aware of how long the hug had lasted. "Thank you," he murmured.

"Anytime." She patted his face. "Now, introduce me to your friend."

"Sean, meet…" Rider looked to Jalissa's grandmother.

"You can call me Gran."

"Gran," he continued. "Gran, this is my friend Sean. He puts up with me on my off days. Uh, I'm a firefighter so I have weird shifts." Rider gave himself an inward shake. Did she need to know that?

Sean grinned. "He'd have no life without me."

Gran laughed, slapping her thigh. "I bet you're right, young man. Have you fixed yourself a plate?"

"No, ma'am."

"Go on, then. Make sure you fill 'er up. We don't raise no skinny kids round here."

Rider held back a chuckle at the wide-eyed excitement on Sean's face.

"Is that okay?" Sean whispered.

"Sure is." Rider squeezed his arm in reassurance.

"Thanks, Gran," Sean called as he took off for the table full of various offerings.

"Sure thing, baby." She turned her gaze on Rider. "Where did you meet him at?"

"I mentor him through a program called SAFE. Helps kids who've been bullied."

She nodded. "I thought you were a good one. You have a kind smile."

Her compliment loosened something inside him. He cleared his throat. "Did you get a plate yet, Gran?"

"Oh, no. I like to watch the kids get a plate first. I don't want to get in anyone's way. These ol' bones are mighty slow at my age."

"How about I fix a plate for you?" His gaze jumped to Jalissa when she gasped. "I can fix one for you as well?"

Her cheeks reddened. "No, thank you." She added enough frost to cool the temps by ten degrees.

"Girl, let that boy fix you up a plate." Gran sank into a nearby chaise. "Some children act like they have no sense."

Rider bit the inside of his cheek to keep from laughing at the salty expression on Jalissa's face. Clearly, she didn't appreciate her gran's sentiment. He put on an expression of innocence. "It's no problem at all."

Especially if Gran would do all the work of irritating Jalissa for him.

"Fine. A little bit of everything, please."

"Sure thing."

He whistled all the way to the table. He filled up both plates, making Gran's portions a little bit smaller. She was a slight thing and didn't look like she'd eat a whole lot. He grabbed some napkins, then trotted over to the ladies.

"Here you go, Gran." He passed her the food, then gave Jalissa her plate. "Hope I got enough of your favorites."

"This is perfect." Gran shooed him away. "You make sure to grab you a plate or two and let that sweet boy get a second helping."

Rider chuckled. "I'm sure he's already hoping no one notices if he eats another round."

"Growing boy, huh?"

"Yes, ma'am. His mother was just saying he's grown out of last year's winter clothes."

Gran leaned forward, maintaining eye contact with Rider as she got close. "Now you listen here."

"I'm all ears."

"You're doing a good thing helping him out. Make sure you take care of his practical needs as well. I've already told Jalissa I'd buy whatever fund-raising offerings you two come up with."

He spared Jalissa a glance, surprised she'd tell her grandmother about working with him. Rider refocused on Gran, lightly squeezing her hand. "You're a gem."

"You best believe it."

Rider laughed, then grabbed some food before settling down next to Sean. "You on your second helping?"

Sean's cheeks darkened. "Sorry."

"Nothing to apologize about. I just figured you ate the first plateful before I could sit. Besides, Gran said to eat your fill."

"She did?" Sean peered up at Rider.

"Promise."

His shoulders sagged, and he fiddled with his napkin. "Rider?"

"Yes?" He paused before taking a bite of a beef rib.

"Do you think it would be okay to take a plate home with me? For my mom?"

Rider's heart turned over. Were they low on groceries again? He tried to buy double of items he knew Sean liked and let him take things home onesies-twosies style, since Sean's mom didn't like accepting help. But maybe that was no longer enough. "Yeah, bud. That'll be just fine."

"Thank you."

They ate in silence, then Sean looked at Rider. "Everyone here is so nice. Are all families this way?"

Good question. His mom's side of the family was practically nonexistent. She had one brother but her parents had passed already and there were no aunts and uncles. His uncle Jay—his mom's brother—had never had any children.

"I think so."

A contemplative expression came over Sean's face. "I want this one day."

At that moment, Rider could completely agree with the sentiment.

Chapter Seven

Jalissa's knuckles turned white around the steering wheel as she neared the firehouse. Whimpers and hissing sounded from the crates in the back of the animal shelter's van. The noise only added to her already fried nerves. Since Flo was harnessed, the dog couldn't comfort Jalissa from the passenger seat.

So she dragged in a deep breath and slowly exhaled while thinking of palm trees and smoothies served in coconuts. A trip to the beautiful state of Hawaii topped her bucket list and served as her peaceful destination to imagine when tension passed regular levels and headed for the stress and worry arena. Every payday, she moved some of her funds out of her checking account and into her savings. Yet she still hadn't saved enough money to visit the fiftieth state. Minor repairs for her hatchback and other household expenses kept taking a chunk out of her bank balance.

As she imagined the salt breeze from the ocean, tension seeped from her shoulders. But as soon as she put the van in Park and saw Rider sauntering from the bay doors, her pulse ratcheted up a step. Watching the slight swagger in Rider's steps and the easy grin on his lips gave her pause. For a moment, he looked attractive.

What are you thinking?

Apparently, she wasn't. She straightened her shoulders and slipped her mental armor on. Just because Rider had been perfectly charming with her family didn't mean she'd let that soften her toward him. She also wouldn't let the cryptic statement he made at Trinity's regarding his lack of a father change her mind any. He was still arrogant, immature and a touch reckless.

Only counting his flaws didn't silence the questions. She couldn't help but wonder if his father had passed away. Or maybe he was alive and had a new life with a new family. The lack of answers scratched at her like a cat on a post. And how could someone so arrogant wrap Gran around his finger?

"Morning, Tucker," Rider said when he opened her door. "Captain Simms's wife is already here and has set up the perfect spot for the shoot." Rider pointed toward the rear of the van. "Animals in the back?"

"Yes. They're all in crates."

He opened the back doors then shook his head. "How did you survive the ride with all that noise?"

"Found my happy place." And one day she'd see Hawaii in person. She loosened Flo and moved back so the dog could exit the van through the driver's side.

"You know what happiness is?" Rider smirked.

"Hardy har-har." Jalissa rounded the back to start unloading the animals. "Where am I putting them?"

"Oh, don't worry about it." Rider cupped his mouth. "Young, Trent, Barns, come help!"

She wiggled a finger in her eardrum. "I think your voice carries well enough without you shouting."

"Maybe, but I have no idea where they are in the firehouse. Now you don't have to carry the animals. Plus, the guys already know where everything is set up."

"Then I can leave?" She had a load of laundry she could do.

"Oh, no." He tsked at her. "We need your assistance with the animals."

Jalissa slowly inched backward but stopped when Flo nudged her. *One...two...* She could do this. Be near the firehouse for help. She didn't actually have to go *inside*, did she? Flo licked her fingertips.

"All right," Jalissa said slowly. "I'll just stay out of everyone's way unless I'm needed."

"You'll be needed." He stared into her eyes.

She blinked slowly. What was going on with her? First thinking Rider was good-looking, and now they were having some kind of moment. She needed to fix this real quick. "I'm sure. It's not like I can trust you to be competent."

The firemen rounded the back of the van, ignoring her and Rider's conversation. They quietly began unloading the crates.

Rider rocked back on his heels, sliding his hands into his pocket. "Shots fired in, what?" He pulled an arm up to glance at his watch. "Five minutes. Must be some kind of record for you."

"Whatever." She gave him a wide berth and followed the last fireman from the side parking lot to the front of the firehouse.

She inhaled. *One...two...three...four...* Exhaled. *Five... six...seven...eight...* Flo bumped into her hand as if to let Jalissa know she wasn't alone. She buried her fingers in the soft fur as they strolled up the walkway.

"Jalissa, I'm so glad you came," Mrs. Simms said, coming to greet her, arms engulfing her in a hug.

Kind of reminded her of one from Gran but with more exuberance. Jalissa's shoulders dropped. "Hi, Mrs. Simms."

"How are you, dear girl? How's your mama?"

"She's just fine." Jalissa smiled at the older woman. "I saw her yesterday for a family picnic. Helped her make tamales and empanadas."

"Oh, aren't you a blessing to her."

"I hope so." Jalissa owed everything to her mother. It certainly helped that yesterday had been fun—once she'd gotten over the shock of Rider crashing the party. He and her cousins had started a game of ultimate disc. Sean and the other kids had laughed it up as much as the adults.

"Did Rider tell you the plan for today?"

"Uh, no. I forgot to ask with all the unloading of the animals." Aka her avoiding him like he had mange.

Mrs. Simms clasped her hands together. "I got your list of what pets were coming and already know which firefighter to pair them up with. Omar backed the engine outside, and we'll use that for the backdrop." She motioned behind her. "I thought it'd be nice to have one family shot, so Trinity and the girls are coming as well."

"That sounds adorable. Which animal will Omar hold?"

Mrs. Simms tilted her head in concentration. "One of the pups. Ali, I believe?"

"Oh, she'll be perfect." Jalissa smiled. "Tell me who's up first and I'll get the pet ready."

"Here." Mrs. Simms thrust a yellow notepad paper at Jalissa. "I have the order memorized. You can use this and get the guys situated."

"All right, then." Jalissa scanned the contents. Captain Simms was up first, and his wife directed him to pose with Rover.

"Sit, Flo. Relax," she said, giving the command to let the golden retriever know Jalissa would be fine. Being outside and not *in* the firehouse had eased a lot of her tension.

She opened the first crate, and Rover came out, tongue lolling to the side and one eye peeking out from his fur. Once they were positioned, Mrs. Simms coaxed a smile from her husband right when Rover appeared to grin. Jalissa couldn't believe Mrs. Simms had the foresight to bring a block for the large dogs to sit on. Apparently, she wanted the smaller ones to be held in the firemen's arms.

Jalissa kept busy soothing the waiting animals and exchanging one four-legged model for the other. Some of the other firefighters helped, playing with the pups and convincing the cats they were good people. When Trinity and the girls showed up, Jalissa eagerly watched the photo shoot.

The girls looked adorable, wearing matching dresses and pink barrettes in their hair. Mrs. Simms positioned Trinity next to Omar as he held a puppy and the girls stood in front of him, holding their hands up as if reaching for the small dog. Jalissa couldn't help but pray they would actually adopt Ali. Maybe each of the firefighters would be moved to adopt one of the animals, or at least recommend the shelter to their friends and family.

Mrs. Simms called Rider for his turn, so Jalissa grabbed Milo, the adorable gray kitten that had come in a couple of days ago. Next, she scooped up Manny, one of the boxer-mix pups, and shuffled over from the bay to the engine parked outside. Rider chatted with Mrs. Simms, who laughed delightedly. Jalissa stifled the urge to roll her eyes. *Always trying to charm someone.*

"Ah, here she is," Rider said. "How should I hold them?"

"Fold your arms like you're going to hold a baby," she instructed.

He did so, and she placed Manny on the block, then laid Milo in his left arm, ignoring the fresh scent of Rider's cologne. She lifted Manny, then set him on the crook of Rider's right elbow.

"This is almost perfection, but we're missing something," Mrs. Simms exclaimed. Her eyes widened, and a dimple peeked through her round cheeks. "I know! Jalissa, curl your arm around Jeremy's shoulder and smile for the picture."

Jalissa's mouth dropped. "Oh, no, ma'am. I'm not supposed to be in the pictures." She didn't want to close the distance between her and Rider.

"Well, you should be. Y'all put this together, so we're gonna commemorate the collaboration with a picture."

Jalissa didn't want to touch Rider with a ten-foot pole, but judging by the determined look on Mrs. Simms's face, she had no choice. "Yes, ma'am." With a quick thought, she whistled for Flo. "One more okay?"

"Of course, sweetie." Mrs. Simms peered through her lens. "Now, wrap your arm around him."

Reaching an arm around Rider's shoulders was no problem considering her five-nine height. Still, he had about four inches on her.

"Actually, why don't you just lay your head on his shoulder?" Mrs. Simms called out.

Jalissa froze. "I think this is just fine." Her skin already tingled, and she mentally berated herself for not wearing long sleeves today.

"Come on, Tucker. You're not scared of cooties, are you?" Rider whispered.

She squinted her eyes at him. "Finally admitting you're a disease?"

A bark of laughter fell from his lips. "The longer you protest, the longer your arm rests on my shoulder."

She stiffened, then laid her head on his shoulder. Flo bumped against her legs, and Jalissa curled her fingers around the dog's collar.

"Perfect," Mrs. Simms exclaimed.

Rider took care to not move a single muscle. He couldn't. If someone had told him his heart would feel funny in his chest when Jalissa laid her head on his shoulder, he would have laughed them out of the firehouse. How could he have known how wrong he'd be?

The irritation that always prickled the back of his neck whenever she was around was strangely absent. But what had been left in its place was unidentifiable. It was like he'd lowered his guard to see past the tough exterior she presented. Granted, it could simply be her fear of Mrs. Simms he'd observed. Everyone was afraid of upsetting the captain's wife.

"Smile like you're on an epic vacation," Mrs. Simms ordered.

He curved his lips upward, imagining surfing the waves of Hawaii. Something he'd only done once and had been itching to do again ever since.

"Y'all, this might be my favorite picture of the day." Mrs. Simms beamed. "We're all done."

Jalissa moved away from him like she'd been touched with a hot branding iron.

"Thank you so much for this, Mrs. Simms." She'd offered to take the pictures for free as long as they listed her info in the calendar.

"My pleasure, Jeremy. I'll email you once I have the calendar all set up. I know y'all want to do presales. Once you know how many you want my distributor to print, let me know."

"Right." Mrs. Simms had told them how much it would cost to print, so now they just had to come up with the perfect preorder price to cover that total and raise funds for the programs. "I'll talk that over with Jalissa and let you know later."

Now he just needed to find her. She'd left him with the kitten and puppy. Did she forget he was holding them like a first-time dad with twins?

"That'll be just fine. Be sure to help that young lady load all these animals back into her van."

"I will." Despite what Jalissa thought, he *was* responsible. He was the first person to help another in trouble, unlike her. He remembered seeing her staring at him in the halls of their high school. But had she ever tried to save him from his tormentors?

No. He needed to remember that and push all these feelings aside that were calling him to befriend her. Rider walked into the firehouse bay, where the kennels were. Jalissa knelt before a crate, guiding a sheepdog inside.

"Do you need help?"

She peered over her shoulder. "No, thanks. I've got Rover. Just put Manny and Milo in those crates." She gestured to the left, where two crates had been removed from the group.

Rider squatted and looked for markings or something to indicate which animal went where.

"Kitten in the gray crate," Jalissa called.

"Thanks."

The animals went willingly into their crates, and soon he had them both secure. Rider stared down at the puppy. If he didn't work twenty-four on, twenty-four off, he might consider getting a pet. Yet it wouldn't be very responsible of him to let a dog sit alone in his place all day.

By the time he stood, the guys had already started hauling the crates to the van. Rider grabbed his two and followed Barns, placing the kennels inside where Jalissa directed.

"So, hey, do you have time to talk about the next steps?" he asked.

Jalissa bit her lip. "Sure. How about we meet at the Beanery in an hour? I need to get these guys situated first."

"That'll work."

He tapped the back of the van, then walked to his truck. Hopping into the F-150, he drove straight to the Beanery. Even though Jalissa said an hour, Rider figured he could get some reading in or just relax. As he pulled into the parking lot, his cell phone rang through the car's Bluetooth.

"Hello?"

"Jeremy!"

"Hey, Mom." He unbuckled his seat belt and leaned back. What did she want now? She never called for simple pleasantries. "How are you?"

"I'm good. I haven't heard from you in a while."

He winced. "I'm sorry. I've been distracted by this fund-raising business." And a woman with gorgeous brown eyes.

Gorgeous? He blew out a breath. That photo shoot had scrambled his brains.

"How's that going?"

"We just finished a shoot for our fireman's calendar."

"I'm gonna have to order a few of those and send them to my friends."

"That would be awesome." He rubbed his forehead. *Lord, please give me an abundance of grace for my mom. Amen.*

"So, Jeremy, I was thinking…"

"Mmm-hmm?"

"What do you think about me coming down for a visit?"

His mom had moved to Dallas right after Rider had graduated high school, which hadn't been a huge surprise. If it hadn't been for his aunt and uncle offering their help in raising him when Rider had been in his rebellious teen years, his mom would have never moved to Bluebonnet. Being a single mom, she'd jumped at the offer, then griped the entire time.

After graduation, he barely saw her, even though he'd followed her to Dallas to keep an eye on her and enroll in the community college that led him on the path to firefighting. She'd always had an excuse why she couldn't meet up.

Rider rubbed his chin. Maybe, just maybe, he was still sore about her abandonment. Though, could he claim that when she'd raised him? Still, she hadn't visited in a while, usually only coming every few years for Christmas. "That would be cool, Mom." Yet his stomach twisted like wire at the thought.

"I'm so glad to hear you say that. I have someone I'd like you to meet."

His stomach clenched. "Who?" he asked cautiously. His

mom varied between trying to better her love life and interfering with his.

"His name is Harold. He's a doctor. I really, *really* like him, Jeremy. I think you will, too."

A doctor? That was a first. She'd dated a plumber, a mechanic, a car salesman, a physical trainer and a history teacher, if he remembered correctly. But one thing they'd all had in common, no matter their job, was a complete lack of respect for his mother. It frustrated him that she couldn't see her worth. Just because his father had ditched her didn't mean every single man would. Yet she consistently picked the wrong ones.

"Hey, when you come for a visit, maybe you can stop by the firehouse and go to church with me." He held his breath.

"That sounds great, sweetie."

Rider raised an eyebrow. No objection to church? Maybe the doctor was a believer. "Awesome."

They talked for half an hour, then said goodbye. Rider went inside and ordered a coffee and a cookie, then settled into the corner booth, opening the e-reader app on his phone. He'd been in the middle of a good book by Christian author James R. Hannibal and couldn't wait to get back to the world of spies.

"What are you looking at so intently?"

Rider glanced up to find Jalissa watching him, curiosity sparking in those brown eyes. He blinked and glanced at the time.

"Sorry. I was reading."

Her brows rose.

"Yeah, yeah, you're shocked I know how to read."

"I said nothing." Her lips twitched.

"But you wanted to."

She shrugged and sat.

"You going to get some coffee?"

She shook her head.

Rider studied her. "You didn't get coffee last time." He leaned forward. "Do you not drink the world's sweetest nectar?"

She snorted. "I do occasionally."

"So do I. It just so happens it's every occasion."

Jalissa chuckled, and heat spread in his chest. He'd actually made her laugh. A genuine laugh that shaped her mouth into joy and made him want to do it again. *Wait, no. Remember, befriending is bad. You simply want her to turn down the animosity.*

Jalissa curled her long hair behind her ear. "I like to come in for the seasonal drinks. After a week, my craving's fixed."

"You drink coffee four times a year, for a week each time?" That was how often the Beanery offered seasonal drinks.

"Yep."

"I knew you were weird."

She grinned. "Takes one to know one."

"What happens if you want a winter drink in the springtime?"

"Doesn't happen." She shook her head. "My brain is very regimented. It likes what it likes when it's time to like it."

"That sounds a bit stifling." But explained so much. "I imagine you just go with the flow?"

"Pretty much." Rider curved his lips. "Like today. I drove over here after you said you wanted to meet, talked to my mom for a half hour, then sat down to read until you arrived. None of it planned."

She propped her chin on her hand. "What did you talk to your mom about?"

"She has a new boyfriend." Rider settled back into the booth, exhaling. For some reason, Jalissa seemed ready to be nice, and he didn't want to rock the boat.

"Is this the first time she's dated since—"

Was she fishing for details? No way he'd trust her with them. But this last conversation with his mom wouldn't expose any of his secrets. "No." He snorted. "She's never without a boyfriend. But something about this guy seems different. Or at least, I'm praying so."

Her eyes squinted. "What do you mean, you're praying?"

His back stiffened. "I *am* a believer." Why did she always think the worst about him?

"I know that. I see you at church. I meant, why would you pray about that? God doesn't care who a person dates."

Rider sat, stunned by her proclamation, with no clue what to say.

Chapter Eight

Jalissa's gaze fixed on Rider as he stared at her in what could only be described as shock. His ice-blue eyes widened, his mouth slackened and he seemed to be frozen in one spot. She wracked her brain to figure out what she'd said that had been so surprising.

Finally, she simply asked. "What?"

"Do you really believe," he started slowly, "God doesn't care who we date? Who we marry? Who we yoke ourselves to?"

Was he really using ancient language like *yoke*? She pushed down the laughter when she saw the seriousness of his expression. "Actually, no, I don't. I think He's more concerned with people believing in His son. Anything else are the details that divide the church and give us the multiple denominations we have today."

Rider ran a hand through his brown hair. "I'm speechless."

"Tell me what I did so I know how to repeat the phenomenon."

He laughed then shook his head. "I just… I talk to God about everything. And I do mean everything. He probably wishes I'd be silent a bit more. But it brings me comfort knowing He cares about the little things because *I* care about them. So for me to hear you say the opposite…" He shook his head. "My mind is trying not to explode."

She scoffed. "Be serious."

"I am." He placed a hand on the Bluebonnet FD logo. "Believe me. I'm dead serious." He leaned forward. "God cares enough to know how many hairs are on your beautiful head. Why would He *not* care who you dated?"

A rushing noise filled her ears. Had he called her *beautiful*? Could she find the life pause button or even a rewind? Surely, she'd misheard.

"You think I'm beautiful?" Dread filled her stomach as she heard the echo of her own voice. How could she have asked that question out loud? Right now she wished she hadn't left Flo at the shelter, but she thought a quick meeting would be harmless, without a need for her emotional support dog.

Rider's face flushed.

Why did she think that was adorable? *Get a hold of yourself. He's a firefighter. They can't be trusted. Nothing he says can be trusted.*

But she remembered how helpful he'd been earlier that day. How gently he'd handled the puppies and kittens. How kind he'd been when she arrived, her nerves near their breaking point.

"Beautiful? Did I actually say that?" Rider asked. He rubbed the back of his neck.

"You did."

"Huh. Well, like I was saying, God cares about everything you care about. There are plenty of Scriptures that say as much if you ever want to discuss this further."

Jalissa opened her mouth to go back to the beautiful comment but stopped herself. Regardless of how she felt about God's stance on dating, *she* didn't date. It was easier that way. No one to disappoint her or break promises.

"Thanks for the offer, but I'm good."

Rider tapped his thumb against the table.

"Nervous?" she asked.

He stared down at his hand. "Uh, no. Just a way to get the excess energy out."

"Are you an adrenaline junkie?"

"Not really, but I do like to move around and whatnot."

"But you were sitting so quietly with the book when I arrived."

He smiled. "That's because my mind was racing and trying to figure out if the good guys would win."

"I've never seen this side of you before." Part of her wanted to investigate further, while the other was yelling *abort*.

"You never looked."

His words stung, but she couldn't refute their truth. "You're right. I've never been interested in getting to know you." She shrugged. "What can I say? You're a firefighter."

"So it's not just me?"

"You wondered?" Jalissa tried to ignore the uptick of her pulse.

"If someone seemed to hate you for no reason, wouldn't you?"

A dart pierced her heart. She'd been raised better, but something about Rider made her want to use every tool in her arsenal to keep him farther than arm's length. "I don't *hate* you." Just a dislike for him and all he stood for. Still…

"I don't even know you." She paused, then rushed forward to rip off the bandage. "However, I do have a problem with your job."

"Why? Are you adverse to all things that have risk?"

"Not *all* things."

"But a high percentage?"

Jalissa sighed. "Look. My father died when I was thirteen, and it changed me in ways no one else can understand. I've needed to live life a certain way ever sense. Avoiding risk is one thing, but again, not *all* risk. I like to have fun as much as the next person, but I don't need to do anything to invite death to my door."

"And you think I do?" His gaze pinned her to the spot as he watched, waiting for her reply.

She licked her lips. "From what I've seen, you seem to love risk taking and pushing the envelope. I don't need that kind of drama in my life."

He laughed, but there was nothing humorous in the tone. It fell flat. The starkness had her wincing internally.

"I'm not careless, Jalissa, but I'm glad we got this out in the open. At least I know where I stand."

"Rider—"

He held up a hand. "Please, don't start patronizing me now. Let's just get onto business."

"But—"

He shook his head. "I'm sure you have your trusty, dusty notebook in that bag, so let's get to work."

Jalissa did as he asked, but something inside her splintered. She'd hurt his feelings, and for the first time in…who knew how long…she felt bad about her behavior.

Later that evening, Jalissa tried to relax with Flo in the backyard. She threw the tennis ball over and over until her arm begged for mercy and Flo stopped chasing it, panting for water. "Come on, girl."

They headed inside. Flo lapped water as Jalissa poured a cold glass for herself. Then she sat down at her kitchen's eat-in dining table. Her mind reverted back to earlier, to that moment at the Beanery when a flash of hurt had darkened Rider's eyes and pricked her conscience in response.

Since when had her need to protect herself from harm started infringing on other people's right to be treated kindly? Maybe it was because she looked at Rider as larger than life and always carefree that she'd failed to realize anything she said or did could actually hurt him. Now that the veil had been torn, she didn't really know what to do about her feelings.

For the first time since she could remember, she bowed her head and asked God for wisdom.

Rider opened his front door with a practiced smile in place. He'd been praying about this visit since his mom called last week.

"Jeremy!" She wrapped her arms around him, laying her head against his chest. He'd passed her lithe five-seven frame at the age of fourteen, then he'd hit six-one when he turned seventeen and stopped growing.

He returned the hug. "Hey, Mom."

She stepped back, gaze scanning his face as if to assure herself all was well. She tucked a strand of blond hair behind her ear. "You look great, son. How are you?"

"You do, too, Mom." He moved aside and motioned her in. "Where's…Harold?"

"Oh, he checked in to the hotel and went up to his room." She pulled on the hem of her floral blouse. "He didn't want to impose on our time. I told him we'll all go to dinner. That is, if it's okay with you?"

"Of course." He motioned to the sofa. "Do you want something to drink?"

"Oh, no. I'm fine. I had a bottle of water after I checked into my room."

"I thought Harold was checking you two in?"

"We got separate rooms, Rider."

Wow. Was his mom really changing? He didn't want to come across as judgmental and ask, so he mentally embraced the cautious hope that sparked.

"Tell me what you've been up to." She settled into the sofa cushion. A slight smile graced her face, gentle lines creasing with the movement.

His mom looked really, *really* happy. Rider sat down across from her and dived straight into the thick of his life. He told her about Sean and how well the teen had done in school last year and how he'd started ninth grade last month. He talked about work and the guys there, specifically his friendship with Omar. Then he ended with the fund-raiser the mayor had saddled him with.

"Wow." She covered her mouth, eyes tearing up. "You've

grown into such a good man, Jeremy. I'm so glad nothing I did tarnished your future."

"Mom…"

She waved a hand in the air. "Please, let's not pretend like I deserve a mother-of-the-year award. If it weren't for your aunt and uncle, I'm sure you'd be on the news somewhere and behind bars."

Ouch. Yes, Uncle Jay had been a huge help and had kept him from veering onto the wrong path. Still, Rider would like to think that some measure of his own will would have kept him from becoming a juvenile delinquent. He shook his head. It didn't matter. His path had been carved by the grace of God and love of his family.

"I'm glad you're proud, Mom."

"Oh, sweetie, so proud. I've told Harold all about you." Her lips quirked, showing a bit of her overlapping front teeth.

Rider's phone chimed, and he peeked at it before thinking.

Miss 'tude: Popcorn forms are in. Do you want to take them to SAFE and distribute to the kids?

Rider: How about I meet you there? Then you can see what they're all about.

Miss 'tude: When?

Rider glanced at his mom. "Sorry, just texting Jalissa about a fund-raising issue."

Rider: Not today. My mom is in town. Maybe tomorrow?

Miss 'tude: I can come by after work.

Rider: It's a plan.

He slid the phone onto the wooden coffee table.

"Who's Jalissa again?" his mom asked.

"She's working with me to raise money for SAFE and a few other town programs that depend on city funds."

"Hmm." A faraway look settled into her blue eyes. The same color as his.

He froze. "What's that sound mean?"

"What?" She straightened. "Oh, that. I've been noticing your voice changes whenever you talk about her."

"No, it doesn't." It took all his strength to say that with neutrality.

"It does." She nodded sagely. "Do you like her?"

"Not like that." He could still remember the sting of her words. How she'd called him irresponsible and reckless. Well, not those exact words, but the sentiment was there. "She's prickly and bossy and demanding. I can't deal with people like that."

"Your mouth is saying one thing, but I'm not sure the rest of you got that memo."

"Mom, what are you talking about?"

"You're blushing, Jeremy. Our fair skin can't hide the extra flush to the cheeks." She patted her own as if sympathizing with him.

But all she'd done was make him realize that his face *was* heated. Surely from embarrassment and anger at Jalissa's comment, *not* interest. Yes, he'd thought about her a few times in a way a man noticed an attractive woman, but nothing more. As soon as she opened her mouth, her aggressive attitude took away any interest that could have developed.

Though his brain kept bringing the memory of their photo shoot to the forefront, her fiery words yesterday had his heart raising shields to protect itself. Jalissa persisted in flinging insults without even trying to look past her biases. A woman like that would never see him as an equal. She'd hightail it at the first sign of hardship. He'd had enough of women thinking he was all looks and no substance. Dating was more trouble than it was worth, and there was no way he'd put Jalissa on the list as a potential interest. *And wow, are you steeped in this pity party.*

"I think you're mistaken. I'm not interested in Jalissa, and she's definitely not interested in me." He rose to his feet. "Let's go meet Harold. I'm sure he doesn't want to stay cooped up in the hotel forever."

"Are you sure?" Mom walked with him toward the front door. "I really do want to spend some time alone with you, Jeremy."

"Mom—" he laid a hand on her arm "—we're okay. I'll meet your boyfriend, then we can make plans to hang out more. I promise."

Relief deepened the crow's feet around her eyes, and she rose up on her toes to kiss his cheek. "You're a good son."

"Thanks, Mom."

While he was thankful his mom seemed more mature and responsible this trip, his chest still held an ache. Because now he couldn't help but dissect his mother's claim that he was interested in Jalissa. He'd be a fool to have feelings for a woman who'd made it quite obvious she didn't need anyone. Not to mention they weren't even on the same wavelength regarding God's presence in a person's life.

No way could he yoke himself to a woman who thought God just wanted to make sure people made it to Heaven and that was it. Without God, he'd be the delinquent his mom saw in some alternate reality. God had been the perfect example of a savior, had been a friend when Rider had felt alone and had held His arms wide-open when Rider was ready to accept a father's love.

No, he and Jalissa would stick to a work relationship.

Chapter Nine

The SAFE building was an oxymoron: weeds grew in various places throughout the parking lot. The sidewalk in front of the one-story building had broken apart in places, creating jagged pieces and making walking a cautionary tale. And the inside of the building wasn't much better. Everything appeared to be secondhand. Not that there was anything wrong with reusing furniture. Jalissa had grown up wearing secondhand clothes. SAFE headquarters simply didn't make a good first impression. How had Bluebonnet's citizens let teens seeking refuge end up in a place like this? Was the almost dilapidated structure the best they could offer the town's children?

How in the world had it even passed a fire code inspection?

However, all her observations were nothing but a distraction from the real issue: seeing Rider face-to-face for the first time since she'd insulted him. He'd been cordial in texts and other correspondences, but his jokes were absent and his responses brief.

She'd come prepared to apologize, but so far, she couldn't find her co-coordinator. He'd never shown up late to one of their meetings. His truck hadn't been in the parking lot, and a scan of the premises now proved he wasn't inside, either. She bit her lip as she made her way to the check-in counter.

A teen with brown hair and pink tips stood behind the half-door, earbuds in place. The heavy eyeliner around her eyes added to the bored look on her face. When Jalissa reached the front of the counter, the teen flicked her gaze up and down, then straightened.

"Yes?"

"I'm here to meet Rider."

"He's not here."

Jalissa inhaled then exhaled before speaking. "Yes, I'm aware. Do you know when he's expected to arrive? Is it okay for me to wait for him?" She forced a cheerful tone.

"I don't care."

She totally understood the teen's attitude. She'd worn snark like a second skin after her father had passed. But there was something about seeing this surly adolescent already too far gone in the hurt department that fractured pieces of Jalissa.

"I appreciate your help…" Her eyes darted to the name tag. "Nessa."

"Whatevs."

Jalissa shook her head and took a seat at a round table. One of its legs had been propped up by a block. The longer she waited for Rider to arrive, the more she saw. The more she saw of SAFE, the more she wanted to give these kids all the funds she and Rider would receive from the fund-raisers. She had half a mind to talk to the mayor and insist that SAFE be kept on the city's assistance list. No kid should have to fear for their safety or come to a building that could fall down around their ears.

"Sorry I'm late."

Jalissa jumped at the low tone of Rider's voice. He slid into the seat across from her, hair damp and creases lining his forehead.

"Was there a fire?" she whispered. How had she forgotten the dangers of his job? That he could be hurt any time he walked on shift?

"No. I took the day off to spend time with my mom.

She's in town 'to bond.'" His lips twisted ruefully at the air quotes.

"Oh." Her heart throbbed in her throat, her pulse trying to slow now that she knew everything was fine. "How often does she visit?"

"The last time she came to town was five years ago, and it was the longest visit in the history of visits." He ran a hand across the stubble on his chin. "Admittedly, she's much better this go-around, but I can't relax. Waiting for that other shoe, you know?"

His blue eyes pinned her to the spot. Jalissa couldn't have looked away even if she wanted to. Her mouth dried at the implications of his words. She'd rarely seen Rider vulnerable, and right then, the emotion practically leaked from his pores.

"I know." She continued to meet his gaze. "Has she given you any reason to suspect there's something more behind this visit?"

"No, but she never has in the past, either. I've gotten tired of being blindsided."

"Have you prayed?" Jalissa blinked. Had that question really left her lips?

She'd just recently entertained the idea that God cared about the little things. Then again, Rider *did* believe that. So surely it wouldn't be an odd question to his ears.

"Haven't stopped since she said she'd be visiting."

"Has it helped?"

Rider paused, gaze drifting to the ceiling as if considering. Jalissa waited patiently, sensing the need to keep quiet until he broke the silence. His thumbs tapped a beat on the tabletop until, finally, his gaze fell on her face once more. "Yes and no."

"Why no?" What was the point of praying about the little things if it didn't help?

"Because I'm still looking for what doesn't belong. Still trying to figure out her angle."

"And why yes?"

"Because my immediate frustration has gone. I know He hears me and cares about what I'm going through." He straightened in his seat. "And I know whatever *does* happen, God will see me through it."

Jalissa smiled. "Then I think it's more yes than no."

"Ha," he huffed. "I'm thinking you might be right." His mouth quirked to the side. "Thanks for listening."

"Sure." She motioned around them. "So this is SAFE, huh?" She barely held back the chuckle at the double meaning.

"It is. Want a tour?"

Jalissa nodded, and Rider stood, motioning for her to follow along. He showed her the area where kids and their mentors could sit and do homework. The gaming area—which totally shocked her. How could they afford gaming systems but not furniture where the springs didn't poke you in the back? Then again, maybe those electronics had been donated or previously owned as well.

Finally, they ended up at the check-in counter. "And this is Nessa," Rider introduced Jalissa to the moody teen girl.

"Yes. I met her earlier."

"Not officially," Nessa groused.

"As you can tell by her sunny disposition, Nessa is SAFE's greeter and director to all the fun that can be had in these four walls."

The teen was in charge of something?

"There are more than four walls, Rider. Please stop acting old. I doubt your girlfriend would be impressed." Nessa curled her lips.

Jalissa's mouth dropped, but she couldn't figure out why. Maybe because of the surly tone of voice or the fact that she'd been referred as Rider's *girlfriend*. Okay, it was definitely the relationship moniker.

"She's not my girlfriend," Rider objected.

Nessa flicked her gaze to Jalissa then back to Rider. "Whatevs. You like her and she—well, maybe you're right."

Jalissa laughed, stunned by the teen. "You're all right."

Mischievousness glittered in Nessa's eyes. "So is he." She hitched her thumb in Rider's direction. "He grows on you."

"So does mold. That's not an endorsement," Jalissa quipped.

"Ouch." But Rider's mouth had curved in amusement, no hint of hurt feelings in sight.

Jalissa leaned against the counter. "Does he preen around here, or does he leave that at the door?"

"Oh, I stopped that on day one. We weren't cleared to have that much ego around."

"Tell me your secrets, oh wise one." Jalissa could barely contain her laughter.

"Okay, okay." Rider took Jalissa by the hand, dragging her away from Nessa. "That's enough of whatever that kind of collusion was."

"Hey!" Nessa called out. "I thought we were friends."

"But I haven't entered friendly territory with Jalissa, so that exchange remains collusion."

"Then why are you holding my hand?" Jalissa asked.

Rider dropped it as if he'd been burned. "Sorry." He gestured to the table. "Let's talk more about fund-raising and less about me."

She laughed and opened her messenger bag. "Fine. Let's get to work."

Rider couldn't believe it. That was twice he'd heard Jalissa laugh in genuine amusement. Not because she'd managed to fire the first shot in their verbal dispute. Not because he'd done something foolish that caught her interest. Just a genuine camaraderie between them. Was there hope that they could call a cease-fire and act like adults around each other?

He was more than willing to wave a white flag. With the pressure of his mother visiting, he didn't have the mental energy to be on guard against Jalissa and her temperament as well. Still, he was cautious enough *not* to point out how well they were getting along. Last time he'd done that, she'd aimed a barb his way and twisted it enough to deepen the regret of offering an olive branch.

Maybe he shouldn't try again. God knew he was tired of getting burned for every friendly effort he exerted. Yet, he also believed God wouldn't want him to give up.

Lord, I have too much on my mind. Please ease my burden. Please help me know how to navigate these turbulent waters with my mom and Jalissa. Amen.

"I've got two fund-raisers going on right now."

Rider took the paperwork Jalissa passed to him. He skimmed the top paper that explained how the jerky sales would go.

"The high schoolers are doing the jerky sales. One of the volunteers at the shelter got a group of her friends to agree to help. I went ahead and got them all enrolled to sell all the different flavors. The fund-raiser goes on for a month, and we get twenty-five percent of sales."

"That's it?" He thought for sure it would be more.

Jalissa's mouth turned downward. "Unfortunately. That's why we need something that's going to bring in a lot more money and go directly to us."

Rider could agree with that now that he saw what they were up against. "And the SAFE kids?"

"They'll sell popcorn. That fund-raiser is only two weeks, and after that, I'll switch them to the candles. Do you think they'll be up for it?"

"Most definitely."

Her shoulders sagged. "Great. Where are we at on the calendars?"

"Mrs. Simms printed out a mock-up of a flyer we can use to get people interested and start ordering. Once we have enough to warrant a first print, she'll order from her distributor. I told her I'd cover that fee." He pulled out the folded mock-up from his back pocket.

As he unfolded the flyer, he noticed Jalissa staring at him in shock. "What? What's wrong?"

"Do you always fold up paper?"

He stared at the subject in mention, noting the crease from the many folds. "Uh, how else can I get it into my pocket?"

She cupped her forehead with her hand. "Such a travesty."

"All right. Enough with the big words. You can insult me with smaller ones."

She rolled her eyes. "I'm not slandering you. Simply wondering what your vendetta is against paper."

"Nothing. As long as it doesn't start fires, I rarely give it any thought. Unless, of course, I have to take it with me and need a way to carry it." He held up said item, folded it once more along the creases. "It's a newfangled way to transport from one place to another. I slip it into my pocket and voilà…" He held up his empty hands, then dragged the flyer back out of his pocket.

"I'm buying you a folder."

"Then I'd have to hold it. I don't like holding things."

Her lips pursed. "What about your cell phone?"

"Back pocket. Levi's gave me two."

"Your keys?"

"Front pocket. My key ring only has the car and house key on it."

Her mouth dropped open. "But what if you need to write a note?"

Rider pulled his cell out of the other back pocket, unlocked it and pulled up the notes app. "You really gotta catch up with technology, Tucker."

"Whatever, *Jeremy*."

First time he'd been called by his first name as an insult. He flattened his lips to keep from laughing at the consternation that furrowed Jalissa's brow. Back to business.

He slid the flyer across the table. "What do you think? Mrs. Simms said she could change anything we want on it."

She scrutinized the ad. "No, this looks awesome. I can't wait to see the final product."

Rider had to admit, the calendar was pretty charming. He'd seen the mock-up because Mrs. Simms wanted his approval on each picture. He still hadn't gotten the image of him and Jalissa and those adorable pets out of his mind. They'd actually looked like a family—a new one, but a family, nevertheless. He wondered what Jalissa would think when the calendar released.

"I think you'll like it." He hoped. "Mrs. Simms did a great job."

"And you're sure she doesn't want payment?"

"As long as we pay printing fees, she's okay with no payment for the photo shoot or the flyers. She says it's her contribution to the fund-raising efforts."

"Rider!" a voice called.

Rider looked up and caught Sean waving from the entrance. He waved back and motioned for the young man to come over. Rider stood and clapped his mentee on the back. The boy's brown skin glistened with sweat.

"Hey, man. Glad you came."

"Of course! You said it was time to sign up for the fund-raiser." Sean glanced at Jalissa and smiled shyly. "Hi, Ms. Jalissa." He wiped an arm across his forehead.

"Hey, Sean," Jalissa said.

"What do you think?" Sean motioned to their surroundings.

"It's something."

Sean puffed out his chest. "Rider's the best mentor here. I'm glad, because some of the others aren't so cool."

"Sounds like you two belong with one another." Jalissa smiled, censure completely gone from her voice.

"He's been a big help. I finally stopped getting picked on."

"Confidence, right, Sean?" Rider asked. He nudged the youngster in the shoulder.

"That's right. Bullies don't like confident people." They bumped fists. Sean turned to Jalissa. "Do I have to sign something, Ms. Jalissa?"

She grabbed a sheet from her messenger bag. "No. You'll get everyone to fill out this order form. They'll be offered the opportunity to pay online using the QR code. If they don't have a smartphone, then collect cash from them and turn it in to me or Rider. I'll take care of the rest."

"And I have two weeks for this?"

"Yes, sir."

"Great. I'll get started today." Sean looked up at him. "Catch you later?"

"Sure thing, man."

Rider sat down. "Thank you."

"Sure." She gestured toward the stack of sign-up forms. "I didn't realize so many of the kids didn't have access to the internet."

"Yeah, it's a matter of funds for some of their parents. That's why I asked about the old-school method." He winked. "See, paper isn't always bad."

"If those kids bring back a folded-up form…" She shook her finger.

He laughed. "You'll be grateful we got sign-ups."

"Too true." She slid the rest of the forms to him. "Could you see the others get them?"

"You bet."

She sighed. "Well, guess I should go."

Rider hesitated a moment, then pointed to the air hockey setup in the middle of the building. "Want to play a game before you leave?"

Jalissa looked at the empty air hockey table, then back to him. "No. I think it's best I leave on a good note."

He nodded, slipping his hands into his pockets. Rider was glad she acknowledged they'd been cordial but a little disappointed she didn't want to hang out more.

But why? It was always better to end on a good note than to have something enjoyable turn ugly. His thoughts switched to his mom. Did that same philosophy apply there, or was he protecting himself in both cases?

Chapter Ten

The sound of her tennis shoes hitting the pavement fueled Jalissa with every step. Her forehead glistened, and her breath came in short spurts. She glanced at her left wrist, ensuring she'd maintained her pace to stay in the active zone. Her heart rate was elevated in the normal range for her mile run.

Flo barked, and Jalissa glanced up in time to see another person running on the opposite side of the road. Usually, she ran her route without seeing another person besides the occasional car. She lowered her hand to hover over her pocket where she stored mace.

As she neared the other runner, shock slowed her steps until she came to a stop. "Rider?" she called across the street.

He glanced her way, then did a double take, coming to a stop. Pulling out his earbuds, he crossed the street.

"Sit, Flo," she murmured.

"Hey. I didn't know you ran." Using the sweatband on his wrist, Rider wiped his forehead.

"I have to." If she didn't, her anxiety would be uncontrollable. Hitting the road every morning filled her with control and a sense of purpose. Not to mention the physical benefits she and Flo reaped from the activity.

"I don't get to run as much as I'd like. Thankfully, the firehouse has a gym."

She nodded, unsure of what else to say. It seemed strange crossing paths with him when she never had before. "Why are you out running today?"

His brows rose, and his lips twisted to the side. "Honestly? I had to do something. My mom's been stopping by for breakfast every morning and taking me somewhere to 'bond.'" He used air quotes again.

"Making up for lost time?"

"Yes!" He gripped the ends of his brown locks. What were once perfectly mussed strands now stood at attention. "I don't know how to tell her to dial it down without hurting her feelings."

"Maybe tell her you have other plans?"

"Isn't that kind of rude? She did drive from Dallas to see me."

Jalissa was all out of advice. She had a great relationship with her mom and didn't know what to say to the very agitated man before her.

"I just didn't know we were expected to see each other every minute of the day."

Jalissa laughed. "Sorry." She covered her mouth, trying to gain composure.

"My pain is funny to you, huh?" Humor lit his eyes, adding a warmth she'd never noticed before.

"Maybe a tiny bit." She held her thumb and pointer a smidge apart.

"If you're not careful, I'll make you my alibi when I tell her I have other plans."

Jalissa glanced down the street. Her house was on the next block—the end of her route. She studied Rider. "If you promise to do some real brainstorming, I'll feed you breakfast and be your morning alibi."

"For real?" His eyebrow arched, pure skepticism oozing from him.

She waved a hand at him. "Please don't act all shocked. Just know, I have to run all the way home."

"You live on this street?" he asked.

She nodded. "Next block over."

"Huh. To think I'd been passing your home and never knew."

"Good." She faked a shudder. "We're not friends, Rider."

"But we are fund-raising together." He cocked his head to the side. "Come on, don't you think it's about time we call a truce?"

She studied him. The idea of a truce had her reaching for Flo. "I'll think about it. Let's go." She clicked her tongue, and Flo took off at a run next to her.

They jogged quietly, but tension had already begun to build in Jalissa's insides. She'd never run with another person before, least of all Rider. She didn't know how to act. When she spotted her house, she almost wept in relief. The awkwardness threatened to totally undo her. She stopped in front of the stone home, grabbing her foot to stretch her quad. Rider did the same, eyeing the house.

The pale green shutters gleamed brightly next to the white stone of her home. Her espresso-colored front door stood out but matched the two rocking chairs she had on her front porch. She thought her home perfectly cozy. Would Rider?

"Come on in," Jalissa said as she walked up the sidewalk.

"I appreciate this." Rider pulled out his cell. "I'll let my mom know to catch me later."

She nodded, placing her key ring on the hook by the front door after she walked inside. Flo immediately headed for the kitchen. The noisy lapping up of water reached Jalissa's ears. Normally, she'd shower, but having company called for an altering of routine.

Jalissa washed and dried her hands in the kitchen, then immediately grabbed ingredients for breakfast.

Rider walked into the room, setting his phone on the island that also doubled as her dining table. "Is there anything I can do to help?"

"Yes. Take notes. We need more fund-raisers."

"All right." He scanned her home, then grinned. "Mind if I use a notebook?" He pointed to the end table in the living room.

"Sure."

Jalissa scrambled some eggs, adding pepper, seasoned salt and a dash of milk. She already had bacon frying in another skillet.

"What if we put jars in each Bluebonnet business asking for donations?"

"Oh, that's a good idea." Rider sat on a bar stool and began writing. "We could put a catchy phrase like 'Support Bluebonnet Businesses.'"

She rolled her eyes. "So catchy. But won't that raise expectations that all the funds will be divided among the towns' businesses, *not* the funded programs?"

"Right." There was a long pause. "Maybe we can put an asterisk and list the ones we're trying to support instead?"

"Oh, good. Fine print."

He laughed. "Okay, boss, what's next?"

"Who made me boss?"

"I'm pretty sure you did the moment you committed to this."

Sure, Jalissa thought of herself as in charge, but she hadn't realized that Rider did, too. The thought gave her a small moment of pleasure as she turned off the heat to the skillet. She flipped the bacon and grabbed two plates. "How hungry are you?"

"I just ran two miles, so hungry."

Jalissa smirked. "Whiner."

"Excuse me? How many miles did you run?"

"Flo's old."

"Excuses."

Jalissa shook her head. She grabbed some homemade tortillas and warmed them up on the stove. She put three on a plate for herself and three for Rider, then topped them with eggs, cheese, bacon and diced tomatoes. She stopped before adding the last two ingredients.

"Do you like cilantro?"

"Blech. Tastes like toothpaste."

She mimed clutching her heart. "Travesty." *But more for me!* She sprinkled the herb on her tacos. "What about jalapeños?"

"Bring it on."

Jalissa piled some on all the tacos, then slid a plate across the island toward Rider. "Buen provecho."

"Thanks. These look great."

Jalissa sat down next to him.

"Should I say grace?" Rider asked.

"Yes, please."

"Lord, thank You for this food. Please bless the hands that prepared it. Amen."

"Amen."

They ate in companionable silence for a couple of moments. Jalissa reached for her cup before realizing she hadn't poured them anything to drink. She wiped her mouth. "Thirsty?"

"Water is good."

She set her cup back down and grabbed two bottles from the fridge instead. "So, fund-raiser."

"Yes. Um. Maybe a silent auction? Or host some kind of dinner to bring in funds?"

"Bluebonnet's not a fancy-dinner kind of place." Though the idea held some merit.

"Doesn't have to be fancy. Maybe something cheap and easy to make." Rider took a bite of his last taco.

"Maybe somehow combine the auction and dinner?" She stared out the window. "What could we give away?" Her mind whirled, trying to find the right item.

"Auction a chance for kids to ride in a firetruck? Or adults."

"Hmm…" Her thoughts spun, and goose bumps popped along her arm. "What if we auction dates?"

Water sprayed all over the island. "What!"

The idea was outrageous. Rider stared at Jalissa, who sat there at her breakfast table looking nonplussed. He grabbed a napkin and wiped the water that had spewed from his mouth like H2O from a fire hose. His mind scrambled to come up with a rebuttal that didn't sound like he thought her idea ridiculous. They'd come a long way, and he didn't want to go back to the earlier days of antagonism.

"You haven't said anything," she said.

"I'm kind of speechless."

"In a good or bad way?"

He hesitated, gaze following the lines in her granite countertop. "I'm not sure it's a good idea." He drew in a breath and turned in his seat to face her fully. "Doesn't that cross a line?"

"What line?" Jalissa folded her arms, her brown eyes darkening as if ready to snap fire.

"I mean, what are the parameters of the date? Who would you ask to participate? What will the townspeople think? Your mom? *My* mom?" He ran a hand through his hair and paused for breath.

"A date is when two people meet at an agreed location for social entertainment with the hopes that the interaction will lead to a potential relationship. Nothing more, nothing less."

Yep. He'd gotten her good and riled up. Should he take a stand and pray she'd see his point of view or cave for the sake of peace?

He opened his mouth to speak, but she held up a hand.

"As for who would participate? The singles of Bluebonnet. I'm sure there are plenty of people in town who would like to make a romantic connection, or at least have a chance at friendship. It would be even better if we could widen the pool of candidates to the county and include nearby towns."

Jalissa didn't seem like she had the need for oxygen like he did, so Rider waited patiently for her to answer all his questions, begging his mind to listen and not prepare a rebuttal argument.

"Then again, county citizens might not participate if there isn't a benefit for them. Or they might just because the idea of a date is more alluring to singles," she muttered. "The citizens should be overjoyed that we have such dedication to our city to raise money for local programs and rush to support us. The people should be happy we're doing all of the hard work. And as for my mom..." Jalissa slipped her cell from her leggings' pocket. "I'll call her right now and see what she says."

His neck heated, imagining what her mom might think. She'd been really nice to him at the picnic. If she was anything like her daughter, would that change? And why did that idea bother him so much? "That's not necessary."

"No, no. You're the one that brought mamas into this."

"Not like that." He vaguely took note of the whine in his voice. But seriously, if she thought he would call his mom next, she was mistaken.

After all, this impromptu meeting was supposed to help him *avoid* his mom.

"Hola, mija, cómo estás?"

Jalissa's mom's voice filtered into the room. "Bien, Mamí. Hey, you're on speakerphone."

"Oh? Hello?"

Rider's face heated when Jalissa motioned for him to speak. "It's me, Rider."

"Jeremy, how are you, sweetie?"

"Good, Mrs. Tucker."

"Fantástico. Are you two planning?"

"Yes, Mamí." Jalissa speared him with a glare. "Rider and I are thinking about doing a date auction. Let the Blue-bonnet singles get a chance to win a date and contribute to a good cause. What do you think?"

"Oh, mija, that sounds wonderful."

Jalissa stuck her tongue out at him, and Rider resisted the urge to laugh.

"Will you have bachelors of all ages?"

Her mouth dropped open, and Rider choked trying to cover the laugh that slipped through. He took a sip of his water in time to catch another glare from her brown eyes. He mimed an innocent expression and mouthed *what?*

"We haven't gotten that far in the discussion."

"Well, get a few men in my age group and I'll happily support the cause, mija. I have to go now. See you later?"

"Adiós." Jalissa pursed her lips.

"So." Rider leaned his forearms on the island. "Guess we'll have bachelors and bachelorettes of *all* ages, won't we?"

"Bachelorettes?" she echoed.

"You did say Bluebonnet singles, right?"

She nodded.

"And a single woman is a bachelorette, correct?"

She frowned.

"So like I said. All age groups? Men and women?"

"Fine," she snapped.

And she was back. But this time, Rider was prepared for her snark. He stood, gathering the dirty dishes, and headed for the farm sink in front of the window.

"I'll wash these, then get out of your hair."

"Leave them," she groused. "I'll wash them later."

"No, no. You cooked. I'll clean. Besides, think of it as a thank-you."

"Fine. Then I'll write down people who are single while you clean."

It didn't take that long to clean the dishes, and soon Rider had them dried as well. He peeked through the white cabinetry looking for the right spot to shelve the plates. Afterward, he hung the dish towel where he'd found it and grabbed his cell.

"Thanks again for breakfast."

Jalissa shrugged one shoulder, her face in perfect concentration as she continued to list names.

"I'll see you later?"

"Later. Say hi to your mother for me." She glanced up, her warm brown eyes meeting his gaze. "Are you going to run tomorrow?"

"I am. I have the next two days off."

"I leave at six."

He eyed her, rocking back on his heels. "Is this your offer of a truce?"

"Take it or leave it."

"See you tomorrow at six."

Rider left the house, petting Flo goodbye on his way out. He didn't know what to think about the past hour. The one thing he could decide on, he was glad they'd called a truce. It was one less thing for him to worry about. And one less burden to carry.

Chapter Eleven

Flo sat patiently waiting as Jalissa locked the front door. For the past two days, she and Rider had run her one-mile loop, returned to her house to eat breakfast and continued working on the date auction. Jalissa had secured the community center next month to host the event. Rider had asked his single friends if they would sign up. So far, they had a total of ten participants, four women and six guys. Still, it would look better if they had an even number between the sexes and a variety of ages, so they were searching for more singles. Her mother had even agreed to help coordinate the dinner portion of the evening.

The other night, Mamí had come over for dinner and asked an inordinate number of questions about Rider. She'd even hinted that they should date. Jalissa had laughed a good five minutes over the suggestion until her laughter had hinged on despair.

She and Rider would make a *terrible* couple. Her need for control bordered on obsessive, and his lackadaisical attitude would only make her more anxious. She liked order, and he was the very definition of chaos. She was a bit… prickly, and Rider had a personality like an American bulldog in human form. In addition to their contrary natures, Jalissa was determined not to date anyone.

Mamí had struggled with Papí's firefighting shift, especially the disappointment of missed anniversaries and events because he had to work. Sure, there were times when he took leave, but those had been few and far between.

When he died, Mamí had sunk into a depression, and for months, Jalissa had fended for herself.

She would *never* give another man power over her like that. It was bad enough she couldn't make the anxiety go away. She could only imagine what a relationship would do to her mental state.

No, thanks.

Yet her stance didn't prevent her pulse from racing just a tad when she spotted Rider's tall form leaning against his truck. She could tell herself it was the surprise of seeing him and not the turning tide of her feelings.

Rider straightened to his full height as she drew up next to him. "Morning." His low voice sent shivers up her arm.

"Good morning." She nodded at him, then set the pace.

Because if she didn't run, she'd dwell on the errant strand of hair that draped across his forehead. Or how his eyes changed from ice blue with a touch of gray to baby blue with the sunny skies. Or how well he'd gotten along with her family. She'd seen the care he exhibited whenever Sean was around, or Rider mentioned SAFE. Reminding herself he was a firefighter, that he belonged to the group that had deserted her father in his time of need and caused his death, didn't stop her mind from realizing just how kind and loyal Rider was to his friends. Best to keep her mind focused on anything but him on their run.

Then again, maybe she needed to be real with him in order to snuff out any sparks between them. Let reality do its work. "What made you become a firefighter?" she asked in the still of the morning.

Rider glanced at her in surprise. "My uncle, actually."

Now it was her turn to be surprised, though she didn't let it show. "Really?"

"Yeah. My mom moved us down to Bluebonnet when I was a teen, because I'd become a little mouthy. Her words, not mine. Anyway, my aunt and uncle live here and offered to be her village. I left a middle school I had started getting bullied at to arrive as a freshman, where the same thing continued. I was overweight, which would have been enough ammunition, but add on the lack of a father and…"

Jalissa almost tripped. She couldn't imagine an overweight Rider. She'd assumed he looked the same as a kid as he did now. Full of mischief with sparkling blue eyes. Wait…

"You went to Bluebonnet High?" He was only a couple of years younger than her. Wouldn't she have seen him in the halls between classes? How different had he looked back then?

"You don't remember?"

Was that a twinge of bitterness in his voice? "Um, not really."

"Don't worry about it."

But something told her she should. Before she could come up with something to say, he started talking once more.

"Uncle Jay started taking me to the firehouse on his days off and letting me use the gym. He gave me tips on how to handle rude comments and whatnot. Taught me how confidence was the key to success. If it wasn't for him, I don't know where I'd be today."

That explained why he seemed to strut around and preen like a peacock. Maybe his uncle should have dialed back the confidence lessons. Still… "That's awesome you have such a good relationship with him."

Her father's folks lived down near Galveston, so Jalissa hadn't grown up surrounded by family. But they had always been willing to travel north to lessen the distance. If she needed them, the Tuckers would be around in a heartbeat. But that was so different from having family actually living in the same city.

"What about you?" He nudged her arm softly as they

continued running. "Why do you hate firefighters so much?"

This was it. The reason she'd started this line of questioning. The opening she needed to ensure nothing romantic happened between them.

"You don't have to tell me if you don't want to."

"No, I do." She licked her lips. "Just not sure where to start."

"How about the day you knew, without a shadow of a doubt, that you hated firefighters."

She nodded slowly. "That would be the day a liaison for the Bluebonnet Fire Department knocked on our door to confirm that negligence within the department had been responsible for my dad's death."

"What happened?" Rider murmured.

"Dad's main objective in life was always to provide for us. For my mamí and myself. It was just the three of us, because they couldn't have any more children. Dad always said that it didn't matter, because they'd been blessed with me." She swatted at a bug flying in her face. "He always used to say as long as he could provide for us, life was perfectly fine for him. He settled in Bluebonnet simply because he'd been offered a job with the fire department."

"Your dad was a firefighter?"

Jalissa sighed. "Yes. I know you'd think him being a part of the department would mean I loved and respected the men in uniform, but…" She gulped. "It's hard to feel any affinity with a group of guys that let my father die. His partner ditched him when they were clearing a burning building." She swallowed past the lump. "You know the empty lot near the library?"

"By the old grocery store?"

She nodded. "The station responded to a report of a gas leak at Grills—they sold grills, propane and propane accessories. By the time they'd arrived, the building had caught on fire, but only a portion of it. There were reports of people trapped inside. My dad and his partner were supposed to clear the building together, but his partner left him. From what we learned, he went off because he thought the better plan would be to divide and cover more ground."

Rider groaned softly, as if he knew exactly where this was going.

Jalissa slowed to a walk, then stopped to face him. "That firefighter's desire to be the savior, his *arrogance*, killed my father. Yet the department claimed he was new and still trainable. That he was a good man and that something like that would never happen again. They didn't fire him." She shook her head, still not understanding the decision. "They didn't even reprimand him, as far as I'm aware. Every time we tried to get answers, we got blocked. They wouldn't even divulge his name."

She whirled away from Rider, hoping to ignore the sympathy—or was that pity?—in his eyes. She picked up a jog. "So, yes, I can't stand firefighters. I can't stand the ones who are reckless and go rushing in with no regard for the ones who are supposed to be their brothers and sisters in the fight with them. And I can't abide the people who would stand by someone whose negligence cost me everything."

Her chest heaved, and her eyes ran hot with tears. It was good she'd shared this, let the animosity out. Because now he would see. Rider would have to understand why nothing could ever happen between them, and hopefully her heart would remember the facts her head would never let her forget.

Rider wanted nothing more than to offer Jalissa a hug in comfort. The anguish in her eyes, the hurt running salt tracks down her face—all of it begged him to fix the problem. But a hug wouldn't bring her father back, wouldn't resolve her feelings regarding firefighters and wouldn't bridge the divide between them.

These past two days, Rider had begun to hope they could at least have a real friendship. Running together in the morning fueled and calmed him. Laughing over breakfast—or rather, coaxing a few grins from Jalissa here and there— had sparked something in him. He'd believed they could leave anger behind. How wrong he'd been. She didn't even remember him from high school. Had no clue he was the overweight teen who'd been mercilessly tormented by her group of friends.

Not only that, but she had no respect for him as a firefighter. Of course, he couldn't fault her reasons for that. He understood the hurt she felt. But he knew all too well what happened to people holding in hurts—his mom a prime example. She'd been burned by his dad and never recovered. Well, now she seemed okay. But when he was a child, a teen and a young man, he'd had an absent mom. A mom who didn't want to be responsible for a child who looked exactly like the man who'd abandoned her.

What wounds had the death of Jalissa's father caused?

Kind of explained why he'd never seen her in a relationship. Maybe she knew romance wasn't for her, that she'd only take the hurt out on others.

His eyes widened, finally understanding every little dig she'd flung his way. *Wow.* Friendship was definitely out of the question. Nothing more could ever happen between them.

He gulped. "Thank you for telling me."

She studied him, gaze boring into his. "You understand?"

"I do." All too well.

"And this…" Her voice trailed off as she gestured between them.

He'd fill in the blanks where she couldn't. "We're temporary coworkers."

Her shoulders fell, but she nodded with a steady resolve. Jalissa turned back to the road and started running once more. Rider fell into step beside her, his mind going a hundred miles a minute. He didn't know what else to say or do. This was a problem that held no human solution.

Lord, the hurt Jalissa is carrying around is more than I could've ever imagined. I don't know what to say to her, and I don't know how to help. I'll never be what she needs or wants, and for my own sake, I can't befriend her. I can't be overlooked again. But she obviously needs friends who can help. More importantly, she needs You. You called us friend, Lord. Please show Jalissa that You can be all she needs so she'll unload the burdens she's been carrying.

Rider paused, thinking of what else he wanted to pray. His footsteps matched the rhythm of his breathing, and his skin turned clammy.

I need to pray for my relationship with my mom. I know this. I can sense it deep in my gut, but honestly, I don't know what words to pray. Please show me. Please help me with any unforgiveness I'm harboring. Please help my unbelief. Amen.

They continued the run in silence until they crossed Jalissa's threshold. Rider went to the guest bathroom to wash his hands. Afterward, he grabbed her notebook and some pens and opened to the tab that listed the auction information.

A local event planner had donated materials to decorate the community center for the auction after hearing what he and Jalissa had planned. They still needed more men and women who were willing to be vulnerable and go on dates with other Bluebonnet singles. Rider and Jalissa had to work behind the scenes, so they weren't up for auction.

"Do we have an update on the other fund-raiser sales?" Rider asked, turning to the page in question.

"Yes. The popcorn sales earned us five hundred dollars."

More than he'd imagined. "And the jerky?"

"Those numbers will be coming in sometime today."

"Great." But it didn't feel that way. They were a long way off from their goal of ten thousand.

Jalissa slid a plate across the island to him. "Hey, I decided to go ahead with the adoption event at the shelter."

"Okay." He thanked her for the napkin. "When are you going to have it?"

"In a week. I was wondering if the SAFE kids wanted to volunteer to help. Animals can be really great companions." She pointed to Flo, who was enjoying a bowl of kibble.

"Yeah, I can coordinate with Belinda. I'm sure she'll know which kids would be interested."

"Great."

Rider nodded, but his insides felt hollow. He couldn't quit repeating her confession over and over in his mind. He ate quietly, contemplating the morning's news. Jalissa sat in silence next to him. Perhaps lost in her own thoughts?

He stood. "Hey, thanks for breakfast. I need to go run some errands before I start my shift."

"Sure. I'll keep you updated on any pertinent info."

"'Preciate that." He tipped an imaginary hat. "Later."

Rider's main errand was a much-needed talk with his uncle. He drove to the edge of Bluebonnet proper and turned down a dirt road. His uncle's property was the last house before leaving Bluebonnet. Dust kicked up as he drew closer to the pale yellow ranch house sprawled on flat acreage.

Boomer howled a welcome when Rider climbed the porch steps, but the hound dog didn't budge. Rider bent over to rub him behind his ears. The old dog had lost most of his eyesight and didn't move except maybe to eat.

Rider opened the screen door and rapped on the wood a couple of times before twisting the doorknob and walking in. Aunt Mara and Uncle Jay never locked their door. Always said if they didn't know the person, then the shotgun resting over the mantel would give the intruder pause.

Rider chuckled at the thought and called out, "Anyone home?"

Uncle Jay didn't have a garage. Just a carport that was hidden behind the house. Rider hadn't bothered checking the outbuilding, knowing his uncle was never far away.

"In the kitchen, Jeremy," his aunt called.

He walked down the hallway and turned into the kitchen. "Hey, Aunt Mara. How are you?" He wrapped an arm around her shoulder.

"Good. Mwah." She smacked a kiss on his cheek. "How are you?"

"All right."

"Hmm." Her blue eyes assessed his. "You've got that groove in your forehead. Something bothering you?"

"Yeah. Wanted to talk to Uncle Jay about it."

She motioned toward the door leading out of the kitchen into the backyard. "He's tinkering in the shed."

"Again?"

"Always."

"Thank you." He walked over to the sliding door and paused, eyeing the shed in the back. "How long has he been back there?"

"About an hour. If you time it right, the bread will be ready in another hour." She winked, sliding a pan into the oven.

"Cinnamon or banana?"

"Cinnamon swirl, your favorite." Her grin widened. "God must have known you'd stop by."

"He's good." Rider strolled across the backyard. He didn't believe in coincidences, so he'd accept the blessing of his aunt baking his favorite bread when God knew he'd have something heavy on his heart.

Thank You.

The door creaked in protest as Rider's eyes adjusted to the dim lighting in the shed. His uncle sat in a wooden rocking chair, whittling on a log. He spared a glance in Rider's direction and gestured toward an empty chair.

"Hey, Uncle Jay."

"Jeremy." His uncle nodded in that no-nonsense way of his. "What brings you by?"

Rider slumped back in his seat, letting out a huff of air before spilling his thoughts about Jalissa needing a friend and the death of her father—omitting the details of how he died. More than likely, his uncle would know who her father was. The Bluebonnet Fire Department wasn't that huge, and many retired members still lived in the area. Jalissa deserved his discretion since she'd shared her story in a private conversation.

Uncle Jay whistled low. "That's a lot."

"Yes, sir." Rider met his uncle's gaze. "What do I do?"

"There's nothing you can do, son. Some people learn by observing. Maybe if you show up for all these fundraising events and continue being friendly, she'll see she's wrong in keeping herself closed off." His uncle lifted a shoulder. "Or she might not. You have to accept that you can't change anyone."

Rider swallowed, an image of his mom popping up in his mind. "What if someone seems like they *are* changing? How do you trust the change's permanent?"

Uncle Jay squinted his gray eyes. "You're not talking about Jalissa anymore, are you?"

"No, sir." He rubbed his hands against his gym shorts. "Mom's back."

Uncle Jay slowly nodded. "She came by yesterday. Looks good."

She really did. That was one of the things that Rider kept holding on to. He'd never seen her eyes so bright or her skin blooming with happiness. Gone were the red eyes, the pallor that had hung around for years. His mom actually *looked* happy.

"I thought she did, too."

"But…" his uncle prodded.

Rider jutted his chin forward. "But she always seems okay until she's not. Though, I can admit Harold's not like her usual boyfriends."

"Agreed." Uncle Jay shook his carving knife in the air. "He's good for her, for one thing."

"You think so?" Rider's stomach tensed. "I want to believe that, but…" But her past wasn't earning any marks in her favor.

"Don't rush the transformation, son. Cheer her on the journey and sit back and watch God work."

Definite words to live by. Only Rider wasn't sure how to live them out.

Chapter Twelve

The shelter was a little hectic today. Adoption day was officially underway. Though Jalissa had some of the SAFE teens assisting her, she still felt the walls closing in. She unlocked her office door, waited for Flo to follow her through, then locked it back up. Sinking to the floor, she concentrated on her breathing. Flo placed her paws in Jalissa's lap, her nose nuzzling Jalissa's face.

"I know, girl." She was trying to take deep breaths but just couldn't seem to get her heart rate to slow or her breaths to even out.

She slid her hands up and down Flo's body. The steady movements and the warmth from Flo began to penetrate the panic. Bit by bit, the repetitive motion cleared the haze of anxiety. Jalissa inhaled as she told her brain she had enough air. When she exhaled, she assured herself that everything was fine. The adoption event would go well, and the teens there to assist would get good work experience out of it.

As she went through her mental exercises and focused on Flo's comfort, the attack slowly ebbed. Later, when her shift was over and Jalissa was in the comfort of her own home, she'd probably crash from the drop in adrenaline. For now, she needed to pull herself together and get the adoptions underway.

As she shifted onto her feet, Flo rose on all fours. Jalissa peeked at the small mirror hanging near her door. Her hair was in place, and her face didn't appear flushed. She looked as fine as she was going to get.

Flo's nails clicked against the concrete as they headed

outside toward the front, where all the kennels had been set up. Jalissa had posted flyers last week and run an ad in the local paper—online and in print. She'd been sure to mention donations were welcome on top of adoption fees. Hopefully that would encourage the town's folk to help the shelter.

"Hi, Ms. Jalissa."

She stopped at the greeting, turning to find the person that matched the voice. As Sean and Rider walked toward her, she forced her lips to curve upward. "Hey, guys. Glad you could make it."

Though her words and tone were cordial, her body coiled, tensing at the thought of seeing Rider once more. She'd hoped baring her soul to him would bring an end to anything outside of fund-raising. Of course today fell into that purview, so she couldn't escape him.

"I've been asking my mom for a dog. She doesn't think I'm responsible enough, so I hoped volunteering would show her." Despite the conviction in his voice, uncertainty filled Sean's dark brown eyes.

"I'll be sure to let her know how much you helped," Jalissa replied.

"Thanks!" His cheeks bunched, looking like round apples with the baby fat that was still clinging to his frame.

"Here's what you can do." She pointed to the open kennel that had the pups. "If someone wants to see one of these guys, you make sure they sanitize their hands before you let them hold a pup."

"I can remember that."

"Thanks, Sean."

He nodded and strolled toward the end of the row. Jalissa turned to Rider and almost jumped at the intensity of his gaze. Was he thinking about the info dump she'd given him regarding her father and her dislike of the firefighting community?

"What?" she snapped. She wasn't trying to be rude, but the power of his stare unnerved her. Sent her pulse racing a little too fast. She wasn't going to panic again, was she?

"You're good with kids."

"Sean doesn't count as a kid, in my opinion."

"Why not?" Rider asked.

"He's practically an adult. How long before he turns eighteen?"

"Four more years."

"See? But kids under ten, now, they're scary."

Rider chuckled. "Whatever you say, Tucker. Where do you want me?" His head swiveled as he looked at her setup.

There were animal playpens positioned along the front of the shelter. They all fit on the sidewalk under the overhang, shading the animals and any potential adopter. Jalissa tracked Rider's movements as she thought of a place to stick him. Preferably some place far from her where he could stay out of her psyche.

"How about helping Val? She'll handle the money exchange and you can track any additional donations."

He nodded. "On it, boss."

Jalissa kept a close eye on the animals and the volunteers as people began to stop by and inquire about the adoption process. Flo stuck with her the whole time. Jalissa hadn't put Flo's work vest on her, because the other animals usually kept their distance if she wore it. Besides, it was enough that Flo was there. Just in case.

"Thank you very much." Rider smiled at the woman who added a twenty to the donation jar.

She declined the tax write-off slip and thanked them for working to save Bluebonnet programs like SAFE. Her daughter was a member of the mentorship program and had begged for a pet when she heard about the adoption event. They were walking away with an Old English sheepdog.

Jalissa walked up and sighed. "I'm so glad Rover got a new home."

"Do you name all the pets?"

She shook her head. "Most of them come with names. The ones that used to belong to another owner. We just name the abandoned ones that come without tags or any form of identification."

Rider couldn't imagine anyone abandoning a pet, but he knew that was a common tale. He looked at all the happy smiles, the eager looks on kids' faces as they gazed up at their parents in hope. He could see why people would feel endeared toward pets, but he wasn't sure why Jalissa was.

"Why the shelter? Why is it so special to you?"

She tucked a strand of hair behind her ear. "This was my first volunteer position. I started coming here as…" She waved a hand in the air. "Doesn't matter the reason. Once I fell in love with the pets, I sought a job here. Then I got a degree in business to make myself more appealing for promotions." She shrugged. "I've never left. Never loved anything more than soaking in the affection the animals are so willing to give."

Rider could understand that. It was one reason he always liked hanging with his uncle and aunt. They'd always greeted him with a hug—more like a pat on the back, in his uncle's case—and were eager to hear, and truly listen, about his day. But staying at their house wouldn't have garnered him a job. It made sense why Jalissa wanted to save the shelter.

"Thanks for sharing that."

"Sure." She nodded as if unsure what else to say or do. "Um, I'll go help the others."

"Right." Couldn't have her hanging around and being friendly, could he?

Stop it. No judgment. I don't see you trying to be kind first. Which was true. His feelings still warred with the hurt of the past. He could forgive her for the barbs she threw at him in the present day—especially since she'd divulged the info about her dad—but what was her excuse for high school?

Ask her.

Rider ran a hand through his hair, then smiled as a man stopped at the register.

"I'm interested in adopting one of the cats for my little girl." He pointed to a young kid holding a kitten.

Val smiled and immediately jumped into the spiel she'd repeated for every potential adopter. Once the gentleman and his daughter walked away with the cat, Rider turned to Val.

"How long have you been with the shelter?"

"About five years. Jalissa is wonderful to work with."

Who would have imagined? *Be nice, Rider.* "That's good." He offered a stiff smile. "She seems to really care about the animals."

"Of course she does. Plus, our boss is great and considerate about letting Flo come to work with her."

He eyed the dog in question. Jalissa did go a lot of places with the golden retriever. "Guess she's her best friend, huh?"

"Oh, she's more than that. She's her support dog."

Rider frowned. "What do you mean?"

Val's eyes widened. "You don't know?"

"Know what?"

"Flo is an emotional support dog. I don't know all the ins and outs, but she does wear a vest and can go in most businesses that would usually prevent other animals from coming in. The only reason she doesn't wear a vest when at the shelter is so she doesn't confuse the other animals."

Emotional support dog? What did Jalissa battle that she had a therapy dog? So many questions ran through his mind until his brain held up a stop sign. He gulped. He shouldn't be talking about this with someone else. It was Jalissa's business, and if she wanted him to know, she would have said something.

Rider quickly reached for a subject change but came up blank. Instead, a customer approached, holding out a folded bill. "For donation," the older woman said.

"Thank you, ma'am." Rider took her money. "Can I get you a tax slip for your donation?"

"Yes, please." He filled out the paper after unfolding the green paper to see a picture of Abraham Lincoln.

Yet the whole time he manned the donation station, his mind kept going to Jalissa and all the secrets she held. She was like an abstract painting—no matter how many times you looked, you couldn't see all the layers underneath.

Did he really want to discover the different levels of Jalissa Tucker? It was easier to stick to his own issues rather than focusing on another, especially her. Regardless, he'd turn his attention to today's agenda: getting the pets adopted. The conundrum that was Jalissa would wait for another day.

Chapter Thirteen

Rider: Calendars are in. Mrs. Simms bought them to the firehouse. Do you want to stop by and see them or shall I bring them on our next run?

Jalissa stared at the message, trying to formulate a reply. Yesterday's adoption event had turned out well. He'd been helpful, and they'd managed to raise a thousand dollars in donations. When she'd gone for a run this morning, her mind had begged her to ignore all thoughts of Jeremy Rider. Instead of recalling how sweet he'd been in helping Mrs. Patel adopt an older cat, Jalissa forced herself to empty her brain of anything that didn't include running. She'd accidentally missed her U-turn spot and run longer than normal. Her health watch had clocked her in for a new record, and Flo had needed extra time at her water bowl.

She glanced at her companion, curled up on the doggie bed in the corner of her office. Flo raised her head as if to check that Jalissa was okay. Jalissa grinned, and Flo rested her head back on her front paws.

Rider: Or I can meet you at the Beanery after my shift. I need to fuel up on coffee before seeing my mom later.

Jalissa: The Beanery!

She winced. Her fingers had flown too fast and added the exclamation point. She didn't want Rider to think she was antifirehouse. *But you are. Besides, what do you care what he thinks? You told him everything to create distance.*

Yet her heart insisted that it mattered what he thought. Regardless of how much effort she put into ignoring his existence, her brain insisted on reminding her of his presence. Even now, she was supposed to be waiting for the arrival of some animals from a closing shelter nearby, and her thoughts were *still* on Rider. Shouldn't she be focusing on fund-raising events?

Rider: One o'clock? Or after work?

It didn't help that his texts were muddling her brain. She eyed the clock hanging in the arrivals area. If she pushed her lunch an hour past normal time, she could grab something from the sub shop after looking at the calendars.

Jalissa: One is fine.

Rider: See ya then.

She stared at his name on her cell phone. The one she'd changed when they'd started running together, no longer thinking of him as the bane of her existence. Only seeing Rider outside of fund-raising activities made their relationship seem more than that of mere coworkers. Personal, even. Maybe she should change it back.

She pressed on the name, selected the editing option, then paused.

Lord, why is being around this man so hard? Why can't I just look at him as I do Omar, the mayor or any other man in my acquaintance?

Probably because none of them made her wish her stance on romance and firefighters was different. But she had to protect herself because no one else would. She certainly couldn't depend on a man to take care of her, especially one who wore the Bluebonnet FD blues.

I'll be stronger, Lord.

She'd already made life better for those around her. Mamí no longer needed to worry that Jalissa's anxiety was out of control or work multiple jobs to take care of Jalissa. She had done all right for herself, going to community college while working at the shelter and making her way up to manager. Yet all her success would disappear in a puff of smoke if the mayor decided to stop funding her sanctuary.

Plus, she didn't want to have to lay off any of her people. She certainly didn't want to look for another job, either. She'd just have to hope the auction brought in more money than they could imagine.

Her head tilted as an idea formed. Maybe Mrs. Simms could do another photo shoot, this time using the singles for the auction as models. A modern-day glamour shot to advertise the benefit auction. She smiled as she wrote the idea into the notebook next to her desk phone. Maybe she could get people to share on their social media accounts as well.

The buzzer for arrivals shocked her from her musings. Jalissa rushed toward the back, the sound of Flo's collar tinkling in the wind—a sign the dog had followed her. She opened the door in time to see Ted from animal control holding two animal crates.

"Morning, Jalissa!"

"Good morning." Though the clock was nearing noon. "How many do you have today?"

"Five. I'll be right back."

She nodded and immediately pulled up the form for incoming pets on the desktop computer. Jalissa grabbed the document slip taped to the outside of the first crate and began inputting the data. Looked like there'd be some new kittens. The mama had been abandoned along with her four babies.

Once Jalissa processed all the new animals, she assigned employees to go through the checklist to make sure they were ready for future adoption. Before she knew it, the clock read ten till one.

"Hey, Val, I'm running to the Beanery for lunch. Do you need anything while I'm out?"

Her assistant glanced up from her desk. "Could I get a frozen mocha with whipped cream?"

"Sure thing."

Val pulled a five-dollar bill from her wallet.

Jalissa waved it off. "My treat."

"You sure?"

Jalissa nodded.

"Thanks!"

Her chest hitched as she walked to her car. So far Rider didn't treat her with pity, and that was a good thing. But what would he say if she walked into the Beanery with Flo wearing her work vest? Would he look at her with sad puppy-dog eyes like someone just took his Milk-Bone? She exhaled and drew in a deep breath.

One...two...three...four...

Flo licked the side of her face, and Jalissa laughed, feeling tightness loosen from around her chest. She didn't need to do her exercises to control the anxiety today since her stress level was at minimum, but the act of breathing and counting slowed her pulse and pushed the what-ifs away. Thanks to Flo, her mood tipped to carefree.

No matter what happened with the meeting with Rider, Jalissa would be her usual resilient self. Just because Rider knew why she disliked the Bluebonnet FD didn't mean it would affect their—what had Rider called it?—temporary-coworkers relationship. Knowing Flo was her therapy dog shouldn't matter, either. Although, she still felt exposed knowing Val had shared such personal information. She'd been apologetic, but still...

Everything is fine. It doesn't matter what Rider thinks.

An open spot right in front of the door waited for Jalissa at the Beanery. She slid her hatchback in and parked, then put the work vest on Flo. Though the temps had cooled, and she could probably leave Flo in the car with the windows cracked, Jalissa didn't want to. Something told her to bring the dog with her.

Anticipation drummed through her. She hoped the calendars were perfect and would be a good moneymaker. Mrs. Simms had insisted all the profit outside of printing costs would go to the city, so Jalissa said a quick prayer for favor.

Rider was in the same spot she'd met him the last time. She wove in and out of the tables and then slid into the chair across from him. Motioning for Flo to lie down, she turned to Rider. "Hi."

"Hey. I see your trusty companion is with you."

Jalissa bit her lip, nodding. "She's wearing her vest. Will it bother you?" She pointed to the food in front of him.

Rider spared a glance at Flo then looked back to Jalissa. "Not at all." He slapped a calendar onto the table. "Are you ready for all this cuteness?"

"I assume you're referring to the calendar." But her mind drifted. Why hadn't he asked any questions about Flo?

"Without a doubt. Please note that I'm in there, so I'm also referencing myself."

She rolled her eyes, but her lips twitched with suppressed amusement. Then she saw the calendar. "Aww." Manny and Milo had made the cover. "They look too cute."

"Agreed."

Jalissa chuckled and flipped the page up to January. Every month pulled words of wonder to convey her joy at how charming each picture was. Omar and Trinity's family was perfect for October. The captain had made November. She flipped to the last page, and her heart stuttered in her chest.

It was her and Rider. *Their* photo. The one she'd managed to push from her memory banks. Rider peered down at her, a small smile curving his lips as Jalissa rested her head on his shoulder, looking peaceful. Her stomach churned. How could they look so…so…so *happy*? Surely it was a trick of the camera.

She didn't even remember feeling tranquil at that point. Had she focused on Hawaii in order to not curl her lip at Mrs. Simms's demand that she pose with Rider? Jalissa wished she could remember in order to push the speculation away.

Flo's collar tinkled, and Jalissa turned to see her friend rise. Her warm eyes studied Jalissa as if asking, *are you okay?* Jalissa swallowed and stroked Flo's head.

"We made December, can you believe it?" Rider asked.

"Hmm."

"I thought for sure we'd end up in the middle." Rider grinned. "Aren't the pics great? If I didn't have such an odd shift, I'd be tempted to adopt Manny in a heartbeat."

Jalissa met Rider's gaze. His blue eyes shined brightly, but he said nothing about them appearing to be a couple in the photo. His focus was totally on the animals. Maybe that's what she should concentrate on as well.

"Maybe you could adopt an older dog." Her voice came out raspy as her mind struggled to maintain a switch in topics. "Or a cat."

His nose scrunched. "I'm a dog fan."

"Me, too." She stared down at the calendar, then quickly shut it. "I'll put a stack of these at the animal shelter for sale. Can y'all sell these at the station?"

"Not much foot traffic besides the occasional octogenarian who stops by with baked goods."

She chuckled, glad they were on even footing once more. Flo lay back down.

"But we can put a few out, just in case. And Mrs. Simms

said she'd put up a direct sale link on her site. I have a couple of boxes in my truck. We can get the teens going door to door as well."

"Sounds good." She forced her mouth upward, but the photo of them branded her mind.

"Are you okay?" Rider's brows dipped. "Is something bothering you?"

Jalissa opened her mouth, her mind stalling. She shot to her feet. "I have to grab some lunch. I'll talk to you later."

"Hey, why don't we go to Hickory's? My treat. I haven't eaten yet."

No, no, no. She needed to get away from him, not spend more time with him. But those weren't the words that came out of her mouth. "Fine. I'll meet you there."

"Got it."

Why had he asked her to join him for lunch? She'd made it loud and clear where they stood. Did he really need a meal at Hickory's just to talk about the calendar more? Rider nodded at Poppy and took his usual booth. Kate came by, and he ordered two sodas.

He peered through the window, noting how loud Jalissa's car was as she drove into the lot. He frowned. She needed to get her vehicle looked at. If it sounded that bad, chances were the clunker wouldn't be running for much longer.

He squinted through the glass. What was she doing? She hadn't moved from the driver's seat since she pulled up. Was she giving herself a pep talk like he'd done when he sat in the booth? Or maybe she was getting Flo harnessed.

When she'd admitted Flo was her therapy dog, he almost blurted the first question that came to mind. *What happened?* Then he hushed his inner voice and waited to hear what she had to say. Because for some reason, he'd wanted her to see he wasn't reckless. That maybe he cared, though the idea of admitting that made his skin feel too

tight. He shifted in the booth and blew out a breath, saying a quick prayer for wisdom. A few moments later, a soft
breeze fluttered his hair and cooled him. He lifted his head
and opened his eyes.

"Don't people normally pray right before eating their
food? You don't even have a drink." Jalissa slid into the
booth as Flo took up sentry by the table.

Rider chuckled. "Maybe I like to pray in advance."

"It's okay." Jalissa shook her head. "You can just say it
was personal."

"It was."

"See? Not too difficult to admit, was it?"

This woman challenged him at every turn, but this time
her comment pulled a small smile from him. "Oh, very.
I'm a really private person and don't like to share my in-
nermost thoughts."

Jalissa tilted her head, brown eyes assessing. "I actually
believe you, but I don't blame you. Nothing worse than baring the soul and waiting for judgment."

"But what if judgment doesn't come?" he murmured.

She froze, eyes darting everywhere but in his direction.
"I'm not sure what that's like."

"Maybe not. Or maybe you judge first in order to prevent
people from seeing what's really behind the curtain. The ol'
bait and switch." Rider wanted to smack himself on the side
of the head. Going by the deer-in-the-headlights look on her
face, Jalissa was feeling judged right about now. "Sorry."

"Nothing to apologize for." Her lips spread thin. "Why
are we here again?"

Ouch. He wanted to rub the invisible dart sticking out
of his abdomen, but he didn't want her to know he was
wounded. "You said you needed lunch."

"Right."

He waited for her to say something else but heard crick-
ets. He bit back a sigh. "I thought we came to a truce."

"Of a sort." She looked at every spot in Hickory's except for in his direction.

Well, what a way for her to make life between them awkward once more. "How 'bout we play twenty questions to cover this awkward silence?"

Jalissa laughed, mopping at the soda that sprayed from her mouth. "You're not supposed to admit it's awkward."

Rider grinned. "It was the only way I could think of to break the ice." And boy, was he glad she was smiling instead of moping in silence.

"All right then. I'll go first. Favorite color?"

"Black."

"Such a guy answer." She flicked her hair over her shoulder. "Is that really the answer or you just don't care what color you're wearing?"

Rider laughed. "Both. It's my favorite color because I don't care, and it goes with everything." He tapped the table. "My turn. What's your favorite food?"

"I can't choose. I love my mom's tamales. But snacking on peanuts is my thing."

Gross. Who wanted to snack on something that was guaranteed to make you need a glass of water? "Is that what you snacked on today?"

"No. Chips and guac."

"Oh, yum. Now I'm wishing we would have stopped by El Azul."

Her eyes lit up. "They have the best seafood enchiladas."

"I always get the fajitas."

"Interesting." She tapped her chin. "I'd figured you'd be the type to order something different every time."

"Not when it comes to food." When you knew what you liked, why diverge?

"Then what's your favorite?" Jalissa asked.

"Nachos. I'd eat them every single day if given the chance."

"What kind of toppings do you put on them?"

Rider reached for his drink, taking a moment to cool down before answering. Today had been another scorcher as Texas tried to hold on to the summer for as long as possible. Surely once the calendar turned to October it would have to cool down, right?

Wait, what had Jalissa asked? *Nachos.* "Everything. Chicken, cheese, jalapeños, bell peppers, sour cream. Or switch it up and leave off the meat and add guac and salsa."

They moved from question to question until Rider found out that Jalissa had more favorites than he did. She claimed it was because she had to make decisions instead of leaving things up in the air. Rider admitted he didn't care that much to make a decision unless it was absolutely necessary.

"You mean you have no problem leaving things undecided?" Her eyes widened.

"No. That's not what I'm saying at all." He lifted his hands in a *how can I explain this* gesture. "I don't sweat the small stuff, and the hard things I pray about with God."

"How do you determine what's small and what's not?"

Hope filled him at her willingness to listen. "If I think about it more than once or twice, then it probably means more to me." Like whether or not she'd ever count him as a friend.

Is friends really what you want to be? Maybe not but friendship was what he could trust.

"I just don't understand you, Rider."

"Likewise," he quipped back.

Chapter Fourteen

Today, Jalissa had gotten a new arrival in from a family who was moving out of country and couldn't take their pet with them. After processing the new dog, she'd taken another look at his sweet face. She couldn't believe her eyes or the thought taking her mind hostage.

He would be perfect for Rider.

Pongo stared up at her with age-wizened eyes, the black spots on his face faded from the mark of time. He was nine, and according to the records, still in good health, albeit a little slower without the pup energy. He could keep Rider company when he was home from work. Bonus, the dog was house-trained. The only question was what to do when Rider had to work?

Still, she snapped a leash on his collar and led Pongo outside. She'd already texted Rider and asked if she could drop by. She had to admit the urge to run home and change out of her work uniform—polo and khakis—was strong, but she was determined to keep Rider in the coworker status and not move to friends, or more.

So, she'd keep on her polo, leave her hair in a ponytail and bring Rider his present. Which kind of sounded like something a friend would do, but really, her motive was purely business. If Rider adopted Pongo, then she'd have one fewer animal in the shelter and proof to the mayor that people still used their services. Flo looked irritated to share the back seat with the new dog, but Pongo kept sniffing her in interest.

Jalissa turned down the road, looking at the sprawling

land that lay before her. Rider was a little on the outskirts of town, but he still had a Bluebonnet zip code, according to the GPS on her cell. Her mouth dropped as a barn came into view, outfitted with a mailbox and black numbers proclaiming the address. Did Rider live in a *barn*? Though, why should she be so surprised? She watched enough home-renovating shows to know anything could be turned into a house: dumpster, silo or *barn*.

Jalissa pulled up behind Rider's truck, tipping her head back to look at the storehouse that had been painted white while the newly installed windows had been outfitted with cedar-colored shutters. Though judging from the craftsmanship, they might actually be cedar and not just stained to appear that way.

The yard had been xeriscaped with rocks and cacti, giving the front a clean and well-maintained look. Had Rider done the work himself or hired out? Jalissa strolled up the sidewalk, the two dogs ambling behind her, then rang the doorbell. The crisp and clean sound of the standard bell had her exhaling a breath she hadn't known she'd been holding. Why was she so nervous?

She wiped her palms on her pants.

The door opened, and Rider's lips quirked up in greeting. "Hey, there. Who's your new friend?"

"Pongo. He's house-trained." Great, she sounded abrupt and slightly hostile due to her nerves.

"Oh, don't worry. Everything in here is washable." Rider held the door open wide for them to pass through.

She took in the concrete floors, the wide, vaulted ceiling that showcased exposed black pipes. "You have a loft." And a fireman's pole right in the center.

"My office space." He gestured around. "Want a tour?"

"Sure." Her cheeks heated. What must he think of her unabashed curiosity?

He led her to the kitchen, with its stainless-steel appliances and butcher-block countertops. They added warmth to the industrialized look Rider had going on inside. He told her how he'd worked on the house, one room at a time, in between shifts until it was complete. Finally, they ended up in the great room, with Rider offering her a spot to sit.

Pongo lay flat, jaw resting on his paws, with Flo positioned closer to Jalissa.

Rider stared curiously at her. "What brings you by? Is there something wrong with the fund-raisers?"

"No. They're going great." She offered a stiff smile, heart hammering. "I sold all the calendars I had."

"Awesome! I already ordered more from Mrs. Simms when I ran out yesterday."

"That's fantastic." Jalissa sighed in relief. *Thank You, God.*

"So you didn't need to talk about any of the other fund-raisers? Is this a friendly visit, then?" His brows rose in speculation.

"Sort of," she hedged. "I actually wanted to introduce you to Pongo." The Dalmatian's ears perked at the mention of his name. "He's new to the shelter, and he seemed like he'd be the perfect fit for you."

"Me?" Rider pointed toward his chest. "You want me to *adopt* him?"

"Well, yeah. He's nine years old, house-trained, and he's a *Dalmatian.*"

Rider laughed. "Because every firefighter needs a Dalmatian?"

"Obviously." This time her lips quirked into a genuine smile at his obvious amusement.

He threw his head back, laugh deepening. The sound sent goose bumps racing up her arms, as if the shivers would reach straight through to her heart and penetrate the wall built around there.

He wiped at his eyes then leaned forward, resting his

elbows on his knees. "You know I have a demanding work schedule, right?"

"Yes, but I thought since he's a Dalmatian, maybe the station wouldn't mind if you brought him along? Like I said, he's housebroken, so it's not like he'll make a mess there. Or maybe you can even share custody with Sean." Though it would be better if Rider could bring him to work to establish permanency with Pongo and not create any separation anxiety, since he'd already lost one owner.

But Jalissa kept the rest of her thoughts to herself as Rider examined the dog in question.

Pongo sat up as if he could sense the importance of the conversation. He inched forward, practically begging for permission to enter the fray.

"Come here, boy." Rider patted the side of his thigh, and Pongo trotted over. Rider held out his hand, letting the Dalmatian get to know him before stroking the dog's fur.

"He's super sweet," Jalissa added, praying it would be the clincher.

"How about a trial run?" Rider asked after a long pause.

"For how long?" *Please, please, please.*

Rider met her gaze. "I go in tomorrow at noon. If the captain has approved his presence before then, I'll keep him. If not, I'll have to see if Sean could watch him while I'm away."

Jalissa couldn't stop the grin from stealing across her face. "Perfect. You won't be sorry. Trust me."

She'd brought him a dog.

Rider couldn't ignore the pleased expression Jalissa wore any more than he could ignore the pet before him. He scratched behind Pongo's ears, and the Dalmatian rested his chin on Rider's knee. Pongo's breath puffed out as if he was in a happy place and life couldn't get much better.

Something in Rider's chest shifted as he took stock of the situation.

He'd never imagined in a million years Jalissa sitting on his couch chatting about pets or him thinking of the nearest pet store to load up on supplies. Rider cleared his throat. "Will you go with me to the store? Show me what I need?"

Her eyes widened, then her lips curved. "Sure. I'd be happy to help."

Her happy to help? Rider fought the urge to throw a skeptical look her way. Instead he rose and snapped his fingers. Pongo immediately came to his side and followed him to the front door.

"We're going now?" Jalissa called.

"I don't have any supplies to take care of a dog, so, yes."

She chuckled. "I can't wait to see how you fare." She paused in the foyer, meeting his stare.

Rider studied the dark flecks in Jalissa's brown eyes. Somehow, the view became more than a surface appreciation but a need to discover the secrets she held. *Get real. Snap out of it.*

He stepped back and grabbed his keys off the kitchen counter. "We can take my truck," he offered once outside. He shook his head, trying to wipe the memory of her gaze from his mind.

Pongo hopped into the back seat, and Flo followed. Jalissa then moved to open her door before he could offer. Not that he would. This wasn't a date. They weren't like that, despite his mind wandering down the what-if trail. He'd effectively put a stop to it each time.

"Do you know where the pet store is?" Jalissa asked.

"Traverse Street, right?"

"Yes. Next to the feed lot."

As he drove the few miles to the store, Rider stared at the road before him, trying to come up with something to fill the silence. In the end, he kept his mouth shut. Soon they parked and Rider got out, opening the back door for Pongo. He stared down at the dog, who peered up at him.

"Bathroom?" Rider asked, pointing to the grassy area on the side of the front entrance.

Pongo blinked, then ambled over to take care of business. He trotted back to Rider.

"Do I need to leash him?" Rider whispered.

She held up a leash. "This is from the shelter, but I need to take it back with me. Besides, Jake's okay if you don't, as long as you keep control of your pet."

They stepped into the store, and Jalissa peeked around Rider's shoulder. "Pongo seems to be very obedient, so I don't think you need to worry about it. However, add a leash to your shopping list."

Rider peeked at the aisle signs then walked down the one that held leashes. His mouth dropped at the different offerings. "How are you supposed to know which one is the best?"

"There are the simple ones that hook to the collar and ones that adjust around the neck. Usually it depends on how well your dog handles a leash."

Pongo meandered over to a black harness and nuzzled it with his nose.

"Or maybe he prefers a harness."

Rider chuckled. "Guess I should have just asked him what we need."

And oddly enough, Rider did just that. Every aisle they visited, Rider looked at Pongo, asking him which one, and the dog always walked up to a single item. Well, until they hit the food aisle. Pongo stalked up and down the aisle, sniffing each package.

"I think you broke his nose," Jalissa said.

"I didn't do it. Why do they have so many choices?"

"There's some for puppies, organic, dried, wet..." Jalissa pointed above them. "And don't forget about treats."

Pongo sniffed at a blue-and-white package, then sat down and whined.

"I think he likes that one."

"He probably does." Rider hefted the feed over his shoulder, then walked to the cart Jalissa had snagged two aisles back. He slid the food underneath the cart.

"I think that's it," Jalissa said. "That should be good to start your new relationship."

"Never thought I'd call myself a dog owner."

"I think it's the start of a beautiful friendship."

Rider snorted. "You just want me to give the shelter money and prove to the mayor that you guys deserve to be open."

"Ugh." She stopped in the aisle, a hand on her hip. "Did you just X-ray my thoughts?"

He rolled his eyes. "Please. Your scheme was obvious the moment you introduced me to Pongo." Still, it touched him. Softened the part he'd purposely kept hardened when it came to Jalissa Tucker. He thought seeing that picture of them in the calendar had made a crack, but her bringing him a dog had smashed his shield to smithereens.

Not that he would admit any of that.

They checked out, and Rider loaded up the cab of his truck with all Pongo's new belongings. When they got back to his house, Jalissa hopped out of the truck.

"I'll help bring this all in," she said.

"Thanks. I appreciate it."

"Sure thing."

They worked quietly, bringing in the food, bedding and toys for Pongo to play with. For a trial run, Rider sure had purchased a lot of stuff. As he grabbed the gravity bowl for Pongo, a sedan pulled up in his half-circle driveway. He frowned, trying to place the occupants, but the tint on the windshield made it difficult.

The driver's door opened, and Harold stepped out.

Oh. "Hey, Harold."

"Hi, there." Harold rounded the front and opened the passenger door for Rider's mom.

"Hey, son."

"Mom." He gulped. How was he supposed to introduce Jalissa to his mother? His mom would read way too much into the simple introduction that manners dictated.

Jalissa walked outside and paused when she saw his company.

"My mom," he murmured.

"Oh." She took a step back. Flo came up to rest underneath Jalissa's hand.

Rider's mom came up, arms wide to wrap him in a hug. He bent down, rubbing the top of her shoulders. "Hey, Mom."

"You look like you've been busy." Her eyes flickered from his to Jalissa.

He swallowed. "We just got back from the pet store." *Way to make that sound platonic.* He cleared his throat. "Mom, this is Jalissa. Jalissa, my mom."

"Nice to meet you, Ms. Rider."

"Nice to meet you, too, dear. Jeremy told me about your collaboration. Are y'all doing something for the animal shelter? Was that what the trip to the store was about?" She gestured to the bag of food he held over his shoulder.

"Oh, no. Rider—*Jeremy*—is now the proud owner of a dog," Jalissa said.

"Temporary, remember?" He shot her a wry look.

"We'll see." She gave an impish grin and a pat on his shoulder. "See you later."

"Oh, don't leave on my account." His mom placed a hand on her heart. "We were just coming to invite Jeremy to dinner. We'd love it if you'd join us, too."

Rider's eyes flew to Jalissa in time to see the telltale panicked look she quickly vanquished. He watched her inhale slowly. Before, he would have thought the actions benign. Now he saw the way Flo stepped in to reassure her. All the times he'd thought her prickly, she'd obviously been going through an unseen battle.

"You don't have to, you know. I'm sure you're busy." He offered the out, hoping to ease her anxiety.

She lifted her chin. "I'll go."

The steel in her voice sent apprehension down his spine. Was she offended he was trying to help? Only time would tell.

Chapter Fifteen

What was she doing?

And when had Jalissa picked up Rider's nervous tic? Her hands paused from tapping a mindless rhythm on her jeans-clad thigh. Somehow, she found herself back in Rider's truck as he followed his mom and her boyfriend to dinner. They'd left the dogs at his house since dinner would be a brief event—she hoped.

When the mayor had thrown them together, Jalissa had foolishly thought she'd rarely see Rider. She'd fully expected him to relegate all duties to her, and she'd been prepared for that. Not this togetherness. Everywhere she turned, Rider was there.

Granted, she'd initiated today's interaction by bringing him Pongo. Still, she didn't regret the decision. Not with the way the old Dalmatian had stared at Rider with adoration the entire time they'd shopped. No. Her only regret stemmed from the uncomfortable ride to the restaurant—wherever that might be.

"I'm sorry about my mom."

Jalissa glanced at Rider's profile. "You're sorry she invited me to dinner?"

"No." He groaned. "She's going to think we're a couple."

The words reverberated around the cab, inside Jalissa's head and pelted her heart. "Why?" she squeaked.

"We may have already discussed you in that role."

Her stomach flipped backward and crash landed. What did that mean? He wasn't interested in her, was he? *No, of course not. This is simply a business arrangement. He*

asked for a cease-fire, not your phone number for a date.
Although he did have her number, but again, strictly business purposes. Right?

"Your silence is killing me," Rider said.

"Sorry. My mind is going a million miles a minute. Why? How?" She clamped her mouth shut.

"My mom is in love. Whenever she gets like this, she always starts trying to play matchmaker. You have nothing to worry about. I set her straight. Once this thing with Harold passes—or she goes back to Dallas, whichever happens first—she'll stop trying to arrange my life."

It'd be hard to miss the bitterness coating every word out of Rider's mouth, and Jalissa found it even more difficult to ignore. "I'm sorry."

He sighed. "It is what it is."

"But that doesn't mean you like the result."

"Isn't that the truth?" There was a slight pause before Rider continued. "Just know that whatever happens at dinner, I'm sorry. If she embarrasses you or asks impolite questions, know I'm not her parent and didn't teach her those deplorable manners."

Jalissa laughed. "Well, you've met my family. Guess it makes sense that I'd meet yours." Her cheeks heated. Why had she said that? The comment sounded too much like a couple in love's conversation.

"If you really wanted to meet my family, that would include my uncle Jay and aunt Mara."

Jalissa could feel Rider's gaze on her but refused to meet it. "Keep your eyes on the road."

He chuckled. "So, what do you think?"

"Think about what?"

"Want to meet my uncle and aunt?"

She stifled a shudder. "Let's get through this meal first."

"Fair enough." Rider cleared his throat. "And if you

need me to divert attention or help in any way…" His voice trailed off.

"What are you getting at?"

"Well, I mean. You left Flo. So I wasn't sure how things worked when she wasn't around to help. You know, in case of a…"

"A panic attack?" It was out there. Now he knew without a doubt. *You did already tell him about Flo.*

"Right. I wasn't sure what your coping mechanisms were when she wasn't around."

"Counting. Focusing on my happy place. Telling my brain I can breathe or that everything is okay."

"Would holding my hand help?"

No. Her brain practically shouted the answer. "I'm sure I'll be fine."

Rider pulled into the parking lot of Anna's. They served the best Southern comfort food in a thirty-mile radius. Jalissa breathed a tiny sigh of relief that the mental health discussion was done.

"If you wait a sec, I'll open your door." Rider studied her.

Something told her he was trying to send an alternate message through his gaze. "And give your mom more ideas? I don't think so." Jalissa reached for the handle.

"Good point, but remember, I can help you with whatever. 'Kay?"

She nodded, then hopped down from the truck.

Even if she had a panic attack, she refused to hold his hand and give Ms. Rider any more ammunition than her love-filled mind had already imagined. Who knew what she was scheming besides getting Jalissa to join them for dinner? And what exactly had Rider meant when he said he'd set his mother straight regarding their relationship? Had he vehemently rejected the idea of them as a couple?

She pressed a hand against her stomach, brain automatically counting to slow her heart rate. Surely, she wasn't feeling anxious over the thought. She didn't *want* to be with Rider or anyone else. Certainly she didn't think of him like *that*…much. If only she could ignore the kindness that was beginning to stand out. How had she ever thought him pure arrogance?

Harold and Ms. Rider were already waiting inside when Jalissa and Rider walked in.

Ms. Rider stood, beaming at them. "They're getting a table ready."

"Harold, party of four, right this way." The hostess gestured for them to follow.

One…two…three…

"Are you okay?" Rider murmured.

Four… "I'm just fine," Jalissa whispered back.

"Then stop twisting your purse strap."

She glanced down at the crossover strap resting against her front. Her hands held it in a death grip, rotating in opposite directions. She dropped her hands and forced her lips to smile. "Better?"

Instead of responding, Rider motioned for her to sit first. Her eyes widened at the booth bench seat. His mom had requested a booth? A *booth*! She gulped and slid across the brown leather.

Five…six…seven…

"So, Jalissa, Jeremy says you run the animal shelter?"

"I do. I'm the manager."

"That's awesome. How long have you been working there?"

This she could talk about. Familiarity brought an ease to her shoulders. "Since high school. I love it."

"That's amazing." Ms. Rider's grin widened, her light blue eyes sparkling with…

Well, Jalissa didn't know with what.

"I imagine it's a lot safer than Jeremy's job, and that you don't have to fear any injuries."

"Not exactly. I've had the occasional dog bite and claw marks from some of the cats. You know, basic animal injuries."

"Cats are vicious," Rider exclaimed.

Jalissa arched an eyebrow. "Or maybe you just scared one."

"Not my fault it climbed up the tree and didn't want to come down. If you ask me, it was trying to escape its owner."

"You really rescue cats from trees?" She tried to keep the laughter from her voice but failed miserably.

"More than I'd care to admit."

"I'd rather you save cats than fight fires," Ms. Rider interjected.

Jalissa couldn't disagree with that sentiment. No one should get that kind of knock on their door. *Just another reason to maintain a working relationship.* Because even if she could consider Rider a friend, there was that underlying fear that he wouldn't survive his next call. How did Trinity handle Omar's job?

Just then, their server walked up to take their drink orders. Jalissa purposely requested a water, ignoring Rider's look. She didn't want his mom getting any ideas from her ordering the same drink as him. Besides, she could go home and guzzle down all the Big Red she could ever want.

Conversation lulled as they started in on the fried veggies. Jalissa popped a piece of broccoli into her mouth, hoping the action would prevent Ms. Rider from asking any more questions.

"So, Jalissa, are you single?"

Jalissa coughed against the broccoli trying to go down the wrong pipe. Rider patted her back as she reached for her water. Eyes watering as she recovered, she met the wide gaze of Rider's mom.

"I'm sorry," Jalissa croaked.

"Oh, no, dear. I didn't mean to surprise you with the question."

Surprise wasn't the word Jalissa would use, but it would suffice. "It's fine."

"Mom, really. Her personal life isn't any of your business."

Ms. Rider fidgeted with her napkin, a look of hurt in her eyes.

Jalissa bit back a sigh. "I'm single, Ms. Rider. And it's okay if you ask questions." It would have to be. Because she didn't want to hurt the woman's feelings. For some reason, she wanted Rider's mom to like her.

Lord, please help me.

Rider wanted to sink under the table and never surface unless he could figure out a way to fast-forward time and skip this whole ordeal. He couldn't believe how gracious Jalissa was being. She'd answered his mother's questions calmly and with a smile—except for the minor choking incident. After that, she'd seemed to hit her stride. No sign of any tension or anxiety present.

Part of Rider wanted to be irritated with his mother, but he was learning more about Jalissa than if he'd tried asking the same questions himself. He never knew she got her bachelor's degree online while working at the shelter or how she'd gone and done the same to earn a master's. Or the fact that she'd lived in Bluebonnet her whole life but spent most of her summers in Galveston visiting her father's side of the family.

As his mom asked question after question—much to his humiliation—a different picture of Jalissa emerged. And the part of him that had tried to keep her in the aggravating-person category was caving to grace.

But that doesn't mean she'd make a good girlfriend. Or even friend, for that matter. He needed to know the people he chose to be in his tribe would stick around, not cave at the first sign of adversity. Rider had to pray for God to strengthen his defenses and keep his heart safe from a woman who saw him as the enemy.

"What about Rider? I mean, Jeremy?" Jalissa asked.

His ears perked up, and he tuned back into the conversation around him. What were they talking about now?

"Oh, Jeremy was always getting into trouble as a kid." His mom winked at him.

His cheeks heated. *Great.* Somehow, they'd entered into his embarrassing moments while his mind had been on other worthwhile thoughts. Reliving the stuff he'd done as a kid wasn't his idea of good dinner conversation.

"Mom," he warned.

"Pssh, Jeremy, you know I *have* to tell her about the lasso."

He groaned, dropping his head into his hands. Of all the stories, she *would* pick that one. "Please don't," he muttered against his fingers.

Jalissa's light laughter filled the air. "Please do, Ms. Rider."

"Oh, call me Rebecca."

"Thank you, Rebecca."

Jeremy peeked through his hands in time to watch as his mom leaned across the table. Mischief had her grin extra wide. "Jeremy was three when this happened. I remember, because we'd just celebrated his birthday with a pony party a few weeks before the incident." Her voice dipped at the end.

"Fancy."

He could practically hear the smirk in Jalissa's voice. He dropped his hands to spare her a glance. Yep, she was smirking.

"That was all Jay's doing. My brother."

Rider settled back in his seat, waiting for the humiliation to end. Judging by the indulgent smile on Harold's face, the beam on his mother's and the intrigue on Jalissa's, they were all having a good time at his expense.

"Anyway. Rider fancied himself a cowboy after that. He went around with a lasso trying to rope everything." His mom slapped the table. "It was enough to give me gray hairs."

"I can't spot a single one," Jalissa said.

"Oh, honey, that's blond number eight in the hair-dye section."

Rider smothered a laugh, but Harold let his fly free. His mom did have her moments of hilarity.

"One day I was doing laundry. After I had put up the freshly folded clothes, I noticed Jeremy had gone quiet. Let me tell you, a quiet child is a trouble-making child. I raced down the hall, checking his room, the bathroom and then the kitchen and living room. Nothing. I knew he had to be outside, since there was nowhere else to hide in our small place." She shook her head.

Rider's insides tensed as he waited for the shoe to drop.

"Sure enough, he stood in the backyard with the lasso raised over his head. All I could do was watch in horrid fascination as he threw it."

Jalissa gasped. "He lassoed something? Missed?"

Rider felt posed on the edge of his seat as well, even though he knew the ending.

"Sure did. He had my glass vases lined up in a row. He managed to lasso one, and in pulling it close to himself, he rammed it into another and shattered both vases."

Jalissa's laughter filled the booth. In that moment, Rider could see how free from the excess tension she usually carried she was. Right then, nothing mattered but her joy at his three-year-old self's faux pas.

Embarrassment fled and warmth filled his chest at the amusement in her brown eyes. Eyes that looked at him in camaraderie and not disdain.

Who knew he'd wanted a look of approval from her that badly?

Chapter Sixteen

He was back.

Jalissa squinted out the peephole, noticing Rider's figure clad in exercise gear. When she woke this morning, she'd known he'd show. It was his day off, after all. Only today felt different. *She* was different. She'd met his mother and heard some embarrassing stories that made her laugh even now. The laughter they'd shared over dinner the night before had stripped away her shields. Which meant she couldn't go running with him now unless she could re-erect those barriers in the next zero-point-two seconds.

But how?

Rider knocked again, and Jalissa opened the door. Her heart dropped to her toes as she spied Pongo next to him.

"You brought Pongo." She stared, stunned.

"Of course. We're best friends now."

"Captain Simms was okay with him going to the firehouse?"

Rider nodded. "But we're both a little beat. Can we walk instead? I don't think the old boy wants to run today."

Jalissa's lips twitched. "Probably not. I'm sure Flo won't mind a walk."

Jalissa whistled, then heard the tinkling of Flo's collar as she trotted toward the front door. Flo stopped, sitting so Jalissa could clip on the leash.

"Ready?" Rider asked.

Jalissa nodded and locked up the house. Not immediately shifting into a jog left her feeling antsy. Like she didn't know what to do with her arms. She concentrated on swinging her hands beside her, giving her body something to focus on.

"Hey, do you have the total numbers on how much we've raised so far?" Rider asked.

"Um, yes. We've only raised three thousand."

Rider's shoulders sagged. "That's all?"

She nodded. She'd been praying last night after running the numbers, taking a chance that what Rider said was true and God truly cared about the details of their fund-raiser.

"I thought for sure we'd raised more than that," she grumbled.

"Well, you have to factor in the size of the town. Plus, all the businesses are hurting a little bit. More people move away from Bluebonnet than to."

"True," she sighed. "Do you think we'll fail? That SAFE and the shelter will end up on the chopping block despite our efforts?" She eyed him as they headed down the road.

He ran a hand across his chin then looked at her. "It's a possibility. Do you know what you'll do if that does happen?"

No. Jalissa hadn't let her mind wander that trail. But now, with the question posed before her, what choice did she have? "I have no idea. Working at the shelter is all I know." She shifted her gaze from her feet to meet Rider's eyes. "What about SAFE? What will Belinda do?"

She'd gotten to meet the woman who wore all hats at SAFE. She seemed like a genuinely nice person, and Jalissa hated the thought of the kids not having a place to hang out. Providing the youth of Bluebonnet a secure location to get together with their friends was invaluable.

"Belinda's been trying to find donors. If the city removes its funding, she can no longer afford the lease. She's already checked to see if there's a cheaper place to rent but hasn't found anything yet."

"That's awful." Jalissa clenched her hands until Flo nuzzled against her.

She flattened her hand and stroked Flo's head. "You're such a good girl, aren't you?" she asked, looking down at her companion.

"How long have you had Flo?" Rider asked.

"It feels like forever, but I got her ten years ago. My mom and therapist thought she'd be a comfort."

"Looks like they were right."

Jalissa stared at Rider. That was it? He wasn't going to say something derisive? She bit her lip as her brain tried to catalog the pieces that made up Rider.

"I don't get you." She stopped, placing a hand on her hip.

"What do you mean?" He held up his hands.

"I've been trying to figure you out from day one. You flirt with every woman you come in contact with. You're snarky, rude and arrogant. Yet I've seen you help kids less fortunate than you, assist older women and, apparently, rescue cats from trees. How does that all add up?"

Rider crossed his arms, his gaze assessing, as if *she* didn't measure up.

"Maybe if you get your day one on the right date, the pieces will fall together."

"What?" She blinked.

"Are you talking about when we hung out with Omar and Trinity at Hickory's? Or that time in church when you rolled your eyes when I wished you good morning and asked you to pass the sugar? *Or* that time when you forgot your money at the Beanery, and I offered to buy your drink so the line wouldn't be held up?"

With each tick of his fingers, Jalissa's face heated to an alarming temperature of shame.

"Or…" his voice dropped, his words now a mere whisper "…all those times in high school when your friends picked on the fat kid from out of town and you stood around and did nothing? Tell me, Jalissa, which day one are you referring to?"

Jalissa's mouth dropped open as image after image flashed before her eyes. Before she could process or even begin to respond to his questions, Rider did a 180. Pongo followed, sparing a glance over his shoulder. His eyes held a wistful gaze that tugged at her.

But his owner never once looked back.

Why had he lost his cool?

Rider ran a hand down his face, then looked at Pongo. The dog had been staring at him since Rider walked into the house and sank to the floor.

"I sure did word vomit all over her, didn't I, bud?"

Pongo laid his head on Rider's legs and let out a sigh.

"Exactly. I should have just been quiet. Taken her question at face value."

He tilted his head back and stared up at the beams in the ceiling. "But, Pongo, she kept looking at me like I'm the contradictory one. I couldn't let that slide. I had to set the record straight. Didn't I?"

Pongo kept quiet, and Rider had a feeling that was exactly what he should have done. Instead, he'd made things even more strange between him and Jalissa. Their partnership had already entered an alternate universe, considering they'd met each other's mothers but were in no way in a friendly relationship, let alone a romantic one.

None of that negated the fact that he'd lost his cool. That wasn't okay, and he needed to man up and apologize to her. He stood and headed for the front door. Twisting the doorknob, he gave it a yank—then stopped short.

Jalissa stood outside, fist poised to knock on the door he'd opened. "Oh," she gasped.

"Sorry. Didn't know anyone was outside." He swallowed. "Do you want to come in?"

"Please."

Rider stepped aside and motioned for her to enter. Why had she come? *Doesn't matter.* God had provided him the perfect opportunity to apologize. They headed for the living room and took seats across from each other. Their dogs each claimed spots near their respective owners.

"Look, Jalissa—"

"Look, Rider—"

Their uneasy chuckles filled the air.

"Ladies, first." Rider gestured with a flick of the wrist.

"I'm sorry. About high school. I honestly had no clue that was you, and of course that doesn't matter." Jalissa's eyes slid shut, and she shook her head. Her ponytail swung with the motion. "What I mean to say is, I'm sorry I didn't speak up back then. That I didn't publicly denounce their cruelty. Losing my dad at a younger age made high school kind of a numb experience for me." Her eyes squeezed tight. "But that's not an excuse. I told myself I wouldn't make excuses when I came over here to apologize."

"I was coming to apologize to you." Which seemed silly to say, considering what she'd revealed.

Rider couldn't imagine what losing a parent would do to a person. Especially if you looked up to them and respected them. Being abandoned by his father was on a different plane than losing a parent to death—a tragic one, at that.

"Why? I was the one who started it."

"That doesn't matter." He ran a hand over the top of his head. "I shouldn't have spoken to you like that. I told myself I wouldn't bring up the past, but I did anyway."

"I'm glad you did."

"Why?" What good was revisiting something like that?

"Because I can apologize for my part and maybe bring you closure."

Closure. Not a term he'd thought, but one he could understand. "My beef really isn't with you, Jalissa. Yes, I was upset you didn't seem to recall the bullying, but I guess part of me was angrier you didn't remember how long we've actually known each other." Well, they hadn't really *known* one another. "Or at least been in the same sphere."

"You're not invisible," she murmured.

Tension he hadn't noticed before seeped from his shoulders. A lightness loosed in his heart. "Thank you."

She nodded slowly. "And thanks for wanting to apologize to me, even though I don't think you had cause."

"I was angry. I had cause."

"Okay." She looked down at her hands, then at him. "Now what?"

"Now we continue on. Maybe we'll try walking again tomorrow?"

Her lips twitched. "I'd like that. So would Flo. Right, girl?" She ruffled the dog's coat, and Flo preened under the attention.

"Pongo and I will be there."

Jalissa stood, and Rider followed her to the front door.

"I really am sorry, Rider. I should have said something."

He shook his head. "You had your own grief. And eventually my uncle helped me work through my issues."

"The one you said I should meet?"

"The same."

"Does he live in Bluebonnet?"

"Right on the edge." Was she fishing for an invitation? Could he survive another dinner with her and his family? "I usually visit him on an off day. I was going to stop by this Friday. Want to come?"

"Yes."

She waved goodbye, and Rider stood next to Pongo as Jalissa and Flo got in her tiny vehicle.

Rider closed the door and looked down at his new friend. "What just happened?"

Pongo tilted his head.

"Yeah, I don't know, either, buddy." But Rider thought it seemed awfully like a second chance.

Maybe revisiting the past wasn't such a bad thing. He wouldn't use the same word Jalissa had, but he did feel a peace that hadn't been there before her impromptu visit.

Chapter Seventeen

Could life get any more embarrassing?

Jalissa had tried to help animal control when the cat they'd caught had gotten loose. He'd jumped from the back of the van and fled across the field and right up the tree. Unfortunately, there weren't enough low branches to allow Jalissa to climb the tree, which led Val to call the fire department.

"Cat in a tree, huh?" Rider stood next to Jalissa, eyeing the creature in question.

"Don't start."

He nudged her arm. "Did you scare it?"

"Don't!" She pointed a finger in his face, but it was no use.

His lips twitched, then he let out a hardy chuckle. Obviously, he found the predicament funny.

"I don't know why you're laughing so hard. You're the one who has to get him."

"Oh, no." He shook his head. "I'm just here for the laughs. I rock-paper-scissored Young, and he lost." Rider pointed at Omar, who was leaning a ladder against the tree.

"I hope he doesn't get hurt. Trinity wouldn't forgive me."

"Pssh. It's his job. Besides, you didn't make the animal run up the tree. Did you?"

"No," she huffed. She pointed to animal control. "It's his fault."

"How mature we are to point out faults."

"You started it."

Rider arched an eyebrow. Jalissa turned her gaze away

so she wouldn't be tempted to laugh, but she could feel it bubbling within her.

"What a start to the day," she said.

"Hey, at least the others are behaving."

She snorted. Maybe because the pups weren't around to cause mischief anymore. "Almost all the puppies have been adopted except for one."

"Why hasn't he been adopted, too?"

She looked up his tall frame. "He keeps having accidents when people come to pet him."

Rider bent over at the waist, gasping through his guffaws. Jalissa shook her head. *Men.*

He wiped at his eyes. "I should come to the shelter more often. It's highly entertaining."

"Glad to help you out there, bud."

"Wow, someone's snark is out in full force. I don't know how I'll live being called *bud.*"

Jalissa nudged him with her elbow. "Behave."

"Yes, ma'am." But the twinkle in Rider's blue eyes told Jalissa he was all talk and too much play.

Something had shifted between them, and the bite that would normally be behind her words was remarkably absent. She could tell the jesting was all in good fun on Rider's end as well. The thought made her middle flutter.

Not that she'd admit that aloud. Rider had a big enough ego without her adding to it. Then again, the information he'd shared with her yesterday shattered her past preconceptions. Perhaps his present self-assurance was a way to bolster his self-esteem after the hits it took in high school.

She eyed him, trying to be discreet and still look like she was watching Omar descend with the cat.

"Why are you staring?" Rider murmured.

"It's not every day you see a fireman carrying a cat."

"Right. We'll go with that."

She bit the inside of her cheek. Guess she hadn't been

as discreet as she'd hoped. Omar tromped across the grass and held the cat out to Jalissa.

"Thanks, Omar."

"Sure thing. Trinity will be amused I bailed you out."

She rolled her eyes. "Yeah, yeah. You two just keep on laughing it up." She pointed at Rider and Omar.

"It was funny," Rider called as she walked away.

"Call Trinity," Omar yelled.

"Will do," she yelled back.

She reached the back door to the shelter, and Val opened the door. "Everything okay?"

"Yes, kitty is safe and unharmed."

Val let out a breath. "Oh, good. I can't believe how fast he flew into that tree."

"Like hounds were after him," Jalissa quipped.

"Definitely. Maybe he could smell previous animals in the animal control van."

"Most likely. But you're fine now, aren't you?" Jalissa murmured, stroking the gray cat.

His quivering fur lessened as his heart rate slowed against Jalissa's palm. Jalissa knew how frightening life could be and how trauma could impact the body, so she continued to pet the newbie until all was well.

Meanwhile, she couldn't help but think how nice it was to see Rider and joke without the usual tension between them. Did that mean something? Did she *want* it to mean something? She never set out to have a relationship. She'd seen the pain her mother went through when her father died. That heartache wasn't something Jalissa wanted to put herself through. Especially considering Rider was a firefighter and a long life wasn't a guarantee in that profession.

But she couldn't shake how happy she'd been when she'd seen his smiling face just now. Or how her heart beat to a new pace when he laughed. The sound had made her lips lift on their own accord.

Yes, things were definitely changing, but she wasn't sure what to think of it all.

Her phone buzzed, and she looked at the incoming text from Rider.

Rider: My uncle asked for us to reschedule dinner. My aunt's sick. Sorry.

Jalissa: No worries. I hope she feels better.

Rider: Thanks. Ttyl?

Jalissa: Yep.

She shoved the phone in her pocket. *You're not disappointed. Not. Disappointed.*

But she hugged the cat closer to her, nevertheless.

Rider climbed the stands of Bluebonnet High School's football stadium. Nothing like a good Friday night game to ring in the weekend. Trinity waved as he neared, and he took a spot near Omar, leaving man space between them.

"How are you feeling, Trinity?"

She rubbed her stomach. "Huge."

"Well, pregnancy agrees with you."

"Hey, hey, hey," Omar groused. "Don't compliment her too much. She is *my* wife."

Rider held in a smirk as Trinity raised her eyebrows.

"Your caveman is showing," she quipped.

Rider laughed. "That it is. Where's Rock?" Omar's other father-in-law—the one from his first marriage—was a football regular. He'd coached the high school team once upon a time before retirement had settled him into the life of a spectator.

"On the sideline." Omar pointed straight ahead.

"And the girls?"

"We were able to get a babysitter." Omar grinned.

But Rider barely paid attention as Jalissa entered his line of vision. His hands grew clammy as she sauntered up the steps, sporting a ready smile as she looked Trinity's way.

"I didn't know she was coming."

Omar sighed. "Are y'all going to fight?"

"What? Of course not."

"Of course not," Omar mimed in a high-pitched voice. "What are you talking about, man? Y'all always fight."

"No, we don't," Jalissa said, coming to stand in front of Omar, a hand on her hip.

She looked feisty, and Rider smothered a grin as Omar fidgeted beside him.

"I'm just saying, sometimes your jokes have a little edge."

"Is that a bad thing?" Jalissa asked.

"Not at all." Omar spread his hands out as if trying to calm a cornered animal.

Jalissa nodded at Rider, then sat on the other side of Trinity.

"What was that about?" Omar asked in a quiet tone.

"What? She said we don't argue." Rider shrugged.

"Nah, that nod she gave you. It was almost as if you guys are cordial, or worse…friends. And I thought I spied you two laughing yesterday."

Rider grinned. "Because that's a crime."

Omar rolled his eyes.

"Seriously, is it bad being her friend?"

"Come on. Y'all are like oil and water. Vinegar and milk." Omar slapped a hand on his forearm. "Friday nights and mosquitoes."

"I'm pretty sure Friday nights and mosquitoes go hand in hand."

"I wish it were cooler. It's October. Where are the fall temps?"

"In the north?" Rider asked.

Omar chortled. "Too true."

"Hey, babe—" Trinity tapped Omar "—I need a snack."

Omar straightened. "What would you like? Popcorn? A cold beverage?"

A ping of wistfulness shot through Rider's heart. He'd given up dreams of having a family. He hadn't been on a date in a few years, always seeming to attract women who wouldn't stick around. Once they realized the risks he ran while putting out fires, the allure of his job vanished, and they never called again.

"I'll just come with you. I haven't made up my mind yet," Trinity stated.

Omar helped her down the stairs, and Rider took a sneak peek at Jalissa.

"How's your aunt?"

"Still under the weather." Rider frowned. She'd looked pretty miserable when he brought over some soup. "My uncle will take her to urgent care tomorrow if she doesn't feel any better. He thinks it's a sinus infection."

"Does she get them a lot?"

"I don't think so." He rubbed the back of his head. "I can't actually remember the last time she was sick."

"I hope it's nothing serious."

Rider nodded, worry snaking through his body. He didn't want Aunt Mara to be fighting some serious illness. It couldn't be the flu, could it? Too early for that. Or was it?

His fingers tapped a mindless pattern as his thoughts flew a hundred miles a minute.

"How's Pongo?" Jalissa's soft voice interrupted his spiraling.

"He's good. Loves being at the firehouse but also loves home, too. Especially if I play fetch with him." The guys at the firehouse had unofficially adopted him as the station's mascot.

A bright smile lit her face, and he had to fight against his jaw dropping. He'd never seen her beam that big or unguarded. He cleared his throat. "How's Flo?"

"She was mad I told her to stay home tonight."

"You didn't want to bring her to the game?"

"She doesn't like the marching band. I tried to remind her." She shrugged. "Dogs. They just don't listen sometimes."

"Or maybe you were speaking a different language."

She shook her head. "You always got jokes."

"Huh, I thought that was more of a fact."

She snickered, and he wanted to high-five himself for making her laugh.

What was *wrong* with him? Since when did he care about making Jalissa laugh or doing anything nice for her?

"Aww, just the two people I wanted to speak to."

Rider turned and saw the mayor settle onto the bleacher behind them.

"Hey, Mr. Mayor," Rider said.

"Jeremy. Jalissa." He cocked his head. "I just realized y'all both have *J* names."

"My mom pronounces it with an *H*," Jalissa quipped.

Ha-lisa. Rider rolled it around in his head. That was just as pretty as the way he'd been saying it.

"Well, I wanted to find out how the fund-raisers are coming. I saw you have that big shindig of an auction planned." Mayor Douglas rubbed his chin. "Surprised me to see you doing a dinner *and* an auction. Can't say I think that's the best go of it, but I did put you young people in charge."

"It'll be great, Mr. Mayor," Jalissa said. "You'll see."

"Yes, well, I'll have to take your word for it. If you can

have an update on how much y'all've raised so far on my desk Monday, that'll be great."

Rider glanced at Jalissa and saw her smile falter, but then she nodded.

"Maybe we can make fund-raising an annual thing, Mr. Mayor," Rider suggested. "It would help keep the city from being in a crunch."

"Hmm. Not a bad idea. I'll talk with our accountant." The mayor tipped his ball cap. "Enjoy the night, you two."

Rider didn't know if the mayor was insinuating anything or just wishing them a goodbye. Regardless, he gave a parting to the mayor along with Jalissa.

She sighed. "He's going to hate how little we've raised."

"No. I don't think he had high hopes in the first place. He'll most likely be surprised we've managed to make as much as we have." At last count, they'd been over three thousand. Still a ways off from the ten grand they were shooting for. "Don't forget, the auction is in two weeks."

"You're right. It's going to be the money winner."

Rider prayed that was so. They'd been able to get more bachelors and bachelorettes. Plus, charging per head for the dinner had to have helped, right? He wanted to save SAFE, the shelter and as many other programs in Bluebonnet as possible. *Lord, please let it be in Your will.*

Chapter Eighteen

The reflection in the mirror showcased how nervous Jalissa was. She'd done her breathing exercises and Flo had been stuck to her like glue since she'd started getting dressed for the evening. Which meant she'd have to use the lint roller to trap all the fine golden hairs from the retriever.

Jalissa had chosen a pale yellow maxi dress to wear to dinner tonight. Despite the fact that she and Rider weren't dating, she still wanted to look nice when meeting his aunt and uncle. She knew how close he was to them and how instrumental they'd been in helping raise him.

And maybe, just maybe, she wanted Rider to notice the extra effort she'd gone to. She'd straightened her hair, found some earrings to go with the dress and donned a pair of strappy sandals to round off the image of casual chic. At least that's the look she was going for.

"Bed, Flo." The golden whimpered but trudged her way to the kennel.

Jalissa grabbed the lint roller and swiped the tape along her legs where Flo had been leaning. Finally she deemed the bottom of her dress dog hair–free. She took one last look in the mirror above her dresser.

"This isn't a date. You're just getting to know a friend a little better." Her heart tripped over the word *friend*. Was that really how she was looking at Rider these days? She almost wished he held a different occupation other than a fireman. Not that that would solve *all* her problems in the relationship arena, but it certainly would clear a major hurdle.

She couldn't even muster up the old irritation at the thought of his blue eyes and full lips that smirked more than they grinned. Ignoring her traitorous thoughts, she grabbed a clutch. She would just pretend that they were the best of friends, without an inkling of any other emotion mixed in. That would be the only way she could survive this evening.

Jalissa checked the time on her slim gold watch. Rider should be arriving any—

The knock on the door made her take a step back. *Breathe. It's not a date.* Right. If she could just keep that thought at the forefront, tonight would go smoothly. She twisted the knob and opened her mouth to greet Rider. The words stuck in her throat.

He shot a grin her way. "Hey."

Her mouth dried out. He looked handsome in a navy blue button-up shirt, rolled at the sleeves, over khaki shorts. Guess he was going for casual chic as well. This was the nicest Jalissa had ever seen him dress.

Or maybe now she was simply allowing herself to notice Rider's good qualities. Like knowing how considerate he was, how loyal and helpful he could be to those he cared about, opened the lock to the emotions she'd kept tucked way.

"Hi," she croaked. She swallowed and tried again. "You ready?"

He slid his hands into his pockets. "That I am. You?"

"Yes."

Rider peered over her shoulder. "No Flo? She can come if you want."

Jalissa bit her lip. "Do you have Pongo?"

"Yeah." He hitched a thumb over his shoulder. "He's in the back of the cab."

Good thing she hadn't locked Flo's kennel. She turned over her shoulder and whistled for her friend. The jingle of

Flo's collar sounded before they saw her round the corner of the hallway and into the living room.

"Want to take a ride, girl?"

Flo barked and followed them out the door.

Jalissa watched Rider hold the back door open for Flo as she settled next to Pongo. He closed the door and moved to hers. Flutters erupted in her stomach. This was too much like a date. Rider holding doors open, picking her up, taking her to meet his family.

It's. Not. A. Date. And that was that.

Right, Lord? Please help me know what's what and keep me centered. I don't need to dwell on something that has no basis in truth.

It would be too easy to go down the what-if path and wonder what a future would be like with Rider. She could no longer list his cocky attitude and arrogance as a deterrent. Getting to know him this past month had made a heavy dent in that argument. But the mere fact that his job would leave her with nothing but disappointments wasn't imagined.

So why are you still thinking about him?

Jalissa cleared her throat. "Tell me about your aunt and uncle."

"Okay." Rider glanced at her then reverted his gaze back to the road. "Uncle Jay used to be a firefighter. He got injured five years ago and decided he wanted to relax and putter around in his shop instead. His words, not mine."

"What does he do in the shop?"

"Mess around with engines. Rebuild cars and sell them at leisure once he's done fixing them up."

"That's awesome." All she could do was check and see if her oil was low.

"Yeah, he enjoys it, and the cash from the sales keeps him and Aunt Mara cared for."

"What will you do when it's time for retirement?"

"That's a good question." He absentmindedly tapped on the steering wheel. "I don't know. I kind of like the idea of going back to school and getting a counseling degree or a teaching degree." He spared her a glance. "Is that ridiculous?"

"Not at all. You're great with Sean, and I know how much time you devote to SAFE. They could probably use access to a counselor as well."

"That's a good point. I should bring that up to Belinda."

"Or go back to school and get the job yourself." She paused. "Does that mean you already have a degree?"

"Yes. A bachelor's in fire science. You have a master's in business, right?"

Jalissa nodded. "My mom was so proud. I didn't think she'd stop crying when I showed her the certificate."

"Did you walk across the stage?"

She shook her head no. "I got mine online, and…" She shrugged. "I guess I felt that walking across the stage didn't matter, because I opted out of the traditional route."

"It's still a success."

"True."

Rider stopped at a sign then turned to look at her. "You don't like attention on you, do you?"

"Not at all."

"Duly noted."

Now it was her time to study him. "What about you?"

"I don't like attention, either, but I can handle it now." He nudged a shoulder upward. "What can I say? High school didn't earn me any favors."

"But you came through stronger."

"Thanks to God and my uncle."

"Then let's meet this uncle of yours." She wanted to applaud herself for sounding carefree. It was a good thing Rider couldn't see the quivering mess that was her stomach. Though this wasn't her normal anxiety tying her in knots, just feelings stemmed from a woman going to meet a guy's family.

Ugh. Not a helpful thought but the truth.

Rider tried to keep a light grip on the steering wheel as he turned down the driveway to Uncle Jay's place. He didn't know why he was so nervous, but he was. Maybe the fact he'd never brought a girl to his family's place— even one with a friend label. Or could be he couldn't help but notice how pretty Jalissa looked tonight. Then again, it could be something else he hadn't been able to dwell on during the car ride over.

He put the truck in Park and opened his door. "I'll let the dogs out."

"Does your uncle have any pets?"

"Just a hound. Boomer's old and won't pay them much attention." But maybe seeing Pongo and Flo would perk the old dog up. It was one reason he'd decided to bring his new friend. That and the puppy-dog eyes staring at him when he'd reached for his keys earlier. It was as if Pongo was reassuring Rider that he'd be good on the trip over.

So Rider had brought him and convinced Jalissa to bring Flo. He was sure the three would have fun and become fast friends. Rider unlatched the gate to the fence around his uncle's house and closed it again after Jalissa and the dogs passed through.

"They'll be fine in the yard. Uncle Jay keeps it tidy, even though Boomer never budges."

The dog barked a greeting from the front porch. "See? Let's go introduce Pongo and Flo."

She nodded, thin lines etching their way onto her forehead.

"Are you nervous?" Rider asked. Because wouldn't that bring some measure of relief if she was? But then again, was it regular nerves, or should he recommend she bring Flo inside?

"What do I have to be nervous about?" Her eyes flashed. "It's not like we're dating."

He held his hands up. "Agreed. I just thought I saw your forehead scrunch up." This time, her bark didn't put him on guard. He understood her defense mechanism now.

She rolled her eyes. "You wish."

And maybe he did, but he certainly wasn't going to admit that out loud after her vehement denial about being nervous. Instead, he smirked at her, hoping to ease any tension she held. "Nah. I'm pretty sure you're the one dreaming about happy-ever-afters."

Her eyes froze, then flashed hot.

Whoa. He hadn't meant to fan her anger to life. "It was a joke, Tucker."

She huffed. "Ha. Right. I'm laughing on the inside."

Somehow, he doubted that, but he was done putting his foot in his mouth. The dogs sniffed each other, sizing each other up. Then Boomer flopped back onto the porch. Rider stifled a chuckle. "You want to bring Flo in?" he asked.

Jalissa shook her head, so Rider knocked on the door.

The hinge squeaked and revealed his aunt in the open doorway. "Jeremy!" She enveloped him in a hug.

He squeezed her shoulders and let go. "Hey, Aunt Mara. You look much better."

She smiled. "I feel much better. Thanks for that soup. It hit the spot." She motioned for him to scoot over. "Introduce me to your friend."

"Aunt Mara, this is Jalissa. Jalissa, this is my aunt Mara."

"It's so nice to meet you, Mrs. Rider."

"Oh, call me Mara, and it's my pleasure." His aunt wrapped Jalissa in a hug.

His stomach dipped at Jalissa's wide-eyed, panicked look. She resembled the cat Omar had dragged from the tree. He'd hoped she'd feel comfortable here, not in need of Flo's calmness.

"Aunt Mara, you might be squeezing too tight."

"Oh—" she let go "—sorry. I love hugs and forget not everyone else does." She stepped back. "Come on back. Jay's in the shop, but he set an alarm and knows when dinner will be ready."

"You okay?" he whispered.

"Just fine," Jalissa responded. She raised her voice. "Do you need any help, Mara?"

"Not at all. You're our guest. But Jeremy—" his aunt pierced him with a gaze "—I left the things out for you to set the table."

He nodded. "Yes, ma'am."

"Have a seat, Jalissa. Can I get you something to drink?" Aunt Mara asked.

"A glass of water, please."

"Great."

Rider walked back to the kitchen with his aunt. "We brought our dogs. I left them in the yard with Boomer."

"I can't wait to meet my new grandnephew."

He laughed and grabbed the silverware. Before he could take a step toward the dining room, his aunt stayed him, a hand on his arm.

"So," she whispered, "is Jalissa really a *friend* or more than a friend?"

His stomach clenched. "We're friends."

"Because that's all you want or…"

"Aunt Mara…" He sighed. "It's complicated."

"Isn't that a status on one of those social media sites?"

He laughed. "Yes. But it really is complicated." It felt like an uphill climb just thinking of Jalissa as a friend. Rider didn't want to cross the bridge to something more. Not when he knew her past and how huge an obstacle his occupation was.

Not to mention women have no trouble walking away from you. He swallowed, trying to ignore Aunt Mara's gaze.

She patted his cheek. "I'll pray God's will be done."

"That's the best thing to pray for." But in the back of his mind, Rider wondered if maybe he should be a little more direct in his own prayers.

He excused himself to set the table while his aunt delivered Jalissa's glass of water. A little while later, Uncle Jay walked in the back door. He washed his hands at the kitchen sink, and Rider slapped him on the back.

"Mara said you invited a friend with you?"

"Yes, Jalissa. She's in the living room. Come say hello."

They entered the big room, and Rider took a seat next to Jalissa on the sofa. He nudged her softly. "Jalissa, this old man is my uncle Jay." He smirked at his uncle. "Uncle Jay, this is my friend Jalissa."

"Nice to meet you, young lady."

"Likewise, sir."

Uncle Jay's eyes squinted. "You look a little familiar. Rider tells me you work at the animal shelter."

"I do. Have you ever been?"

"No." His uncle rubbed the stubble on his chin, and his gravelly voice pitched lower with concentration. "You grew up in Bluebonnet?"

Jalissa nodded.

"Uncle Jay usually never forgets a face," Rider said.

Jalissa smiled. "Then I guess eventually you'll remember where you've seen me."

"It'll come to me," his uncle assured her.

"Well, while your old brain gets to ruminating, let's all eat," Aunt Mara suggested.

They stood and made their way into the dining room. Rider pulled out a chair for Jalissa, pleased by her quiet thanks.

After his uncle said grace, Rider offered the dish of pot roast to Jalissa.

"This looks amazing, Mara. Are those homemade biscuits, too?"

"Of course. Can't have pot roast without biscuits."

Conversation flowed easily while they ate, and the tension in Rider's shoulders slowly seeped out. He couldn't believe he'd been so worried. His aunt hadn't stopped grinning since they'd walked through the door. She kept giving Rider secretive glances, as if she was planning his wedding and writing a love story for the books. His uncle laughed here and there but mostly had a look of focus, as if he was still trying to remember where he'd seen Jalissa before.

"So, the auction is in two weeks?" Aunt Mara asked.

"Yes, ma'am." Jalissa nodded. "We're almost done with all the final details. We have all the bachelors and bachelorettes lined up."

"I heard there was a wide range of ages."

"That was my mom's idea," Jalissa said.

"What does your mom do?" Uncle Jay asked.

"She's a housekeeper at the inn. She used to work a couple of other jobs, but when I turned eighteen and moved out, she only had to worry about providing for herself."

"Three jobs, huh? That's admirable," Aunt Mara commented.

"It was born mostly out of necessity."

Rider wished he could reach over and squeeze her hand. He knew how hard it was for her to open up about her dad.

"Why's that?" Uncle Jay asked. "If you don't mind us prying."

A sad smile filtered across her face. "Papí passed away when I was sixteen. He was a firefighter as well."

Uncle Jay's fork froze in midair. He squinted. "Are you Rodney Tucker's girl?"

Rider's gaze flickered back and forth between the two. Did his uncle have good memories of Jalissa's father?

"I am. You knew him?" She leaned forward as if eager to hear more.

Jay's fork clattered, and his face went ashen.

"Jay?" Aunt Mara reached for his wrist, concern etched into her features.

"I...uh... I did. We...worked together."

"Were you friends?"

Uncle Jay shook his head. "I was the new guy. Your dad was experienced, and we didn't have a chance to really develop a friendship before he...before I..." He stood, the chair screeching in protest.

"What's wrong, honey?" Aunt Mara asked.

But Rider could guess the answer to the question. He remembered the venom Jalissa had spewed when she'd told him the reason she hated firefighters.

"It was you?" Rider barely registered his voice croaking like a dehydrated man stuck on an island for a month. All he could think was *not this. Not like this.*

Jalissa gasped, and she gripped the edge of the table.

"Will someone please tell me what's going on?" Mara cried.

"I'm the reason her father died," Uncle Jay rasped.

Chapter Nineteen

Ringing filled Jalissa's ears as the room wavered in front of her. She gasped for air but couldn't drag in a breath. Her skin flushed hot as she placed her shaky hands on her chest.

Then a voice began to replace the bells in her ears.

"Just breathe, Jalissa. Breathe."

She dragged in a breath.

"That's right. Just like that. Take another breath." Rider raised her arms above her head, his eyes capturing hers.

Jalissa could see sympathy crinkling around his eyes, but she was too busy trying to breathe to detail anything more.

"Keep breathing deep."

She complied.

"Good girl. You're doing just fine."

Each inhale filled her lungs more and more until the heat faded and an intense chill clamored for attention instead.

"Aunt Mara, can she borrow a sweater? Uncle Jay, get her dog."

"Absolutely."

Jalissa heard Rider's aunt scrambling away from the table and the slow movements of his uncle.

"Are you okay?" he murmured once they were alone.

She shook her head no. She wanted to get out of there, to go home, but Jay's confession had rendered her useless. Tears sprang to her eyes as what he'd said sank in.

"I'll get you out of here," Rider promised.

Jalissa nodded. Flo's wet nose appeared in her peripheral, and she wrapped her arms around the dog, nuzzling her cheek against the soft fur.

"We're leaving," Rider stated quietly.

"Of course."

Jalissa winced at the sound of Jay's voice and shivered, arms tightening around Flo's body. Her heart pounded.

"Here, dear, take my sweater." Mara thrust it in her face.

Rider took the garment from his aunt and draped it across Jalissa's shoulders. She hated how weak she felt, but not having to do everything for herself in the moment was a blessing. Soon Rider was guiding her out of the house and into the yard.

"I'll leave Pongo here," Rider murmured.

Flo walked so her head was under Jalissa's hand, allowing her to sink her fingers into Flo's soft fur. Jalissa let out a small exhale as the haze around her brain receded.

When she reached the truck, Jalissa hopped in the back seat so she could sit with Flo. The goldie nestled her head onto Jalissa's lap. The comfort of her companion and the warmth from Mara's sweater had Jalissa blinking sleep away as adrenaline faded. No words were exchanged the entire ride to her house. Rider pulled into her driveway and placed the truck in Park.

She quickly opened the door.

"Wait. Let me help. You've had a shock."

Jalissa turned her gaze toward Rider. Concern dripped from every feature, while his hands gripped the steering wheel tightly.

"I don't need your help." She wasn't quite sure why she said it with such force.

He'd guided her out of a panic attack. Made sure she'd arrived safely home. Obviously, she'd been on the receiving end of his aid already. Maybe the shock was wearing off enough for her to feel other emotions. Embarrassment. Shame.

She jumped from the cab, waiting for Flo to get down before shutting the truck door.

But that didn't block out Rider, because he simply lowered the window. "Please call me if you need anything. Anything at all."

Jalissa shook her head. "I think this…friendship has come to an end."

"Jalissa—"

She held up a hand. "I don't need your pity. I don't want your sympathy. Just leave me alone, *please.*" Her voice cracked as the thread that held her together threatened to snap.

A lump in his jaw appeared. "Fine."

She turned and trudged up her walkway. The tears that had threatened since Jay's pronouncement appeared, spilling over in relief of release and bitterness of betrayal.

Jalissa swiped at her face to better see the keyhole, but her hands shook with the force of pent-up emotions. She leaned her forehead against the door, letting out the sobs and the heartache. Flo pressed against her legs, and Jalissa straightened.

She couldn't fall apart out here.

She wasn't sure how she managed to get inside, but hours later—or maybe minutes—her tears had quieted enough for her to hear the knock at the door.

"Coming," she yelled.

Trinity burst through the door shortly after, her stomach leading the way. "Are you okay?"

"How did you know something was wrong?" Jalissa stared at her best friend.

"Rider," Trinity stated quietly. "He called Omar and told him something happened at his uncle's place. Told me to come, so here I am." Trinity studied her. "Are you okay?"

Jalissa ran a hand through her hair. "I feel like my world and everything I knew just got tossed over a cliff. Like someone took an eraser and swiped right through all the parts that would make life make sense."

"Unfortunately, life has never made sense. There are so many events that take place that defy logic and all reasoning. Even though we have our faith, it still doesn't explain away the hurts from the trials we've gone through."

"Then what will? Tell me how it makes sense that a guy I've stopped thinking of as an enemy, maybe even graduated to potential friend—" Jalissa stopped short. If she was honest, her mind had wandered past friendship into more. But that obviously couldn't happen. She swallowed, trying to remember where she'd been going with her point. "Right. Tell me how it makes sense that Rider's uncle is the reason my father died. What will make that hurt less? What will right the wrong?"

"Sweetie, grief hurts. There's no pill to take to erase the pain. But there is a love of a good God, who will comfort us through it. Who will wrap our hearts in love when we think we can't take anymore. He's the one who will be able to right wrongs and wipe away every tear. There is no remedy on earth, but there is the gift of eternal life and freedom when we choose Him. When we choose to step out in faith and believe His truth, *the* truth."

Jalissa sank to the sofa. "How can I walk this earth with this pain? I'm so tired of hurting." She rubbed her eyes, remembering the panic sensation that had stolen her breath earlier.

"I know you are." Trinity sat next to Jalissa, rubbing her back. "But look at your mom. Look at the faith she's exuded all these years."

Jalissa moaned. "How am I supposed to tell her?" She didn't want to cause Mamí any more pain.

"I'll be there with you if you want."

Jalissa leaned her head on Trinity's shoulder. "You're the best."

"You'd be there for me, too."

In the back of Jalissa's mind, she realized the only reason she had a friend with her right now was because of Rider. He'd left her alone but made sure she wasn't actually *alone*. She should probably text him thanks or something, but she didn't want to open the lines of communication with him. Not when the wound was still so fresh and her feelings so turbulent.

Rider knocked on his aunt and uncle's front door once more. He needed to talk to Jay and couldn't wait. He could still picture the shock on Jalissa's face when she realized exactly who Jay was to her. Now that she was home and Omar had agreed to send Trinity over, Rider had had time to explore his own shock at the turn of events. He'd never imagined his uncle would be involved in something like this.

But what exactly had happened?

The door opened, and Aunt Mara's thin face appeared. Her lips were drawn downward, and the lines in her forehead were deeper. "Hey, Jeremy," she sighed, opening the door wider. "Come on in."

"Where is he?"

"Out back. He asked for some space."

"Sorry."

She shrugged. "I cleaned up the kitchen, so I wasn't completely idle."

He winced. "Didn't mean to leave you with all the mess." He always cleaned after she cooked.

"Please—" she waved a hand "—I know you needed to take care of Jalissa. How is she?" Her blue eyes examined his.

"Shook up. She didn't want to talk about it with me, though."

"So she's alone?" His aunt's voice raised an octave.

"No. Her friend is with her."

Aunt Mara's shoulders sagged. "Good." She shuffled into the kitchen. "Want some tea?"

"No, thanks."

"Soda?"

Rider shook his head. "Do you think Uncle Jay would mind if I went out there?" He hitched a thumb toward the backyard.

Aunt Mara bit her lip, her eyes going to the kitchen window that overlooked the yard. "I imagine he thought you'd be back. He owes an explanation."

Rider studied his aunt, wondering how she was handling everything. "Is there anything I can do for you?"

"We'll be fine. We always are." Her gaze shifted to his. "Ups and downs are a part of life and certainly part of a marriage. We'll get past this. I pray you will, too."

Rider nodded slowly. "Maybe direct the prayers Jalissa's way. She needs them the most."

"We all need them, Jeremy. Your hurt is just as important to God as Jalissa's, as mine, as your uncle's."

Rider knew that, but he couldn't shake the thought that Jalissa needed them more. He thanked his aunt and headed for the shed. He scanned the back deck his uncle had built a decade earlier. Uncle Jay sat in a rocking chair staring out at the yard. *Not* in his shed. Rider had no idea what that meant.

"Knew you'd show up," his uncle rasped.

"Had some questions that couldn't wait."

Uncle Jay's gaze pierced him, a haunted look in its depths, and for the first time that night, sympathy churned for his uncle.

"I expected as much," Uncle Jay said. He gestured to the empty rocking chair. "You sit, I'll talk."

Rider did as instructed then stared out at the yard. The sun had made its descent, but the lights Uncle Jay had strung for his wife illuminated the deck.

"I was a hothead in my twenties. I'm sure you can imagine. It's not an unheard-of situation."

"It's kind of hard to imagine you as anything but steady." Rider scratched his chin. "And I thought becoming a firefighter was a decision you made later in life."

"It was, but to understand how I got there, you have to understand my beginning."

Rider slid his hands against his shorts, trying to focus and not interrupt with impatience. Honestly, he just wanted to jump to the part where Uncle Jay had a hand in Jalissa's father's death. That's all that mattered at the moment. But if his uncle wanted to start at the beginning, Rider would give him the benefit of the doubt.

"My dad always got on me about my lack of focus and ambition. I told him that it didn't matter, because I was young. But I drifted into my twenties arrogant and cocky, thinking nothing could touch me. I had a temper, because I expected everything to go my way. Even lived a lifestyle I'm not proud of, but one that no longer holds me in shame. I'm not that man—*boy*, really—anymore.

"I drifted from job to job, greeting my thirties just as aimlessly as I had my twenties. Then I lost my job as a bartender. I didn't have a degree or anything else that made me marketable for a job. I searched the wanted ads, applying to anything that would put food in my stomach. A few weeks later, I saw an ad to become a firefighter. It mentioned on-the-job training and a full-time position. I jumped at the chance. My roommate had gotten married and was moving out soon, and I knew I had to do something."

"How old were you?" Rider asked.

"Thirty-five."

"And you passed the training? The exam?"

"I did. Granted, I still didn't like people telling me what to do. In fact, I had a couple of write-ups saying as much. This continued during my probationary year. After being pulled into the chief's office with a final warning, I managed to prevent myself from getting any more write-ups. I barely made it to my second year. Unbeknownst to me, the guys at the station all requested that I be transferred. Ended up being sent here to Bluebonnet. New year, new place—it was supposed to be a fresh start."

"But it wasn't?" Rider's heart dipped at the bleakness in his uncle's voice.

"No. We got a call about the store smelling of gas. I figured it would be a routine situation. Only when we arrived, the building had already caught on fire. The gas department had shut off the feed to the store, and we were given the okay to search for people. I was tasked for search and rescue with Jalissa's father."

Uncle Jay wiped a hand down his face, his leg beginning to thump up and down with nerves. "I wanted to go left, and he wanted to go right. When I look back, I can see how foolish I was. At that time, I thought I was right, and he was wrong. I wish I could say it was something more profound, but it was stubborn pride that had me splitting apart. I broke protocol and went left, thinking we'd be able to save more people."

A tear slid down Uncle Jay's face.

Rider looked away, giving the older man privacy while he struggled to hold on to his own composure. After a few moments of silence, Rider asked the question burning in his mind. "Why did the department keep you? That wasn't the first time you broke protocol."

"You're right. The only reason they kept me on was the recommendation of the pastor. That was the event that brought me to my knees and turned me away from my selfishness. I sought help from the church. Joined a men's group that was specifically for those who dealt with anger issues and underlying emotions that led to destructive behavior.

The pastor believed I was contrite and could be a better man. The department chose to accept his recommendation."

But his uncle had been too late in turning his life around. Too late for Jalissa and her mother. Yet where would Rider have been if his uncle hadn't changed? The mentorship from this man had saved Rider from a life headed toward destruction. It was obvious that Uncle Jay wasn't the same man who had been reckless. He'd changed.

Just not soon enough to save Jalissa's father.

Rider stood. "I appreciate you telling me this."

"Of course." Jay rose. "I'd like a chance to explain this to your friend."

"No." Rider shook his head. "She's not even talking to me right now. I can't imagine her wanting to hear this from you."

Uncle Jay gulped. "I get it. But when she's ready, you know where to find me."

Rider nodded, then reached out and hugged his uncle. "I'm glad you found God's grace."

His uncle squeezed him, then thumped him on the back. "Go on home. It's late."

And that was as much of a thank-you as Rider would receive.

Chapter Twenty

Jalissa curled her legs underneath her as she settled into the lounge chair. Her mother handed her a bowl of ice cream. "Gracias, Mamí."

Jalissa's mom smiled and took the other lounge chair. "Are you going to tell me what has you so upset?"

"Eventually." Jalissa took a bite of her ice cream, reveling in the coolness of the double-chocolate frozen treat. She could taste a hint of java swirled in the mix.

"Eventually, huh? I may go completely gray waiting for that. Besides, I know you came here to spill."

Jalissa chuckled. "I'll tell you when I'm good and ready, Mamí."

"Oh, so after you eat your ice cream?"

A smirk curved her lips, and Jalissa thought about the same expression that seemed to always be on Rider's face. Then again, it wasn't so much a smirk as a small mark of showing his amusement. Part of Jalissa wanted to text him back. He'd sent another message this morning asking how she was.

She'd typed back a response, then deleted it. Truth was, she didn't know how she felt. Angry, yes. Sad, yes. Relieved, too. Knowing the name of the firefighter who had left her father to his own devices came with a bittersweet relief. If only she could figure out what to do with that information.

She couldn't type all that to Rider, so she'd said nothing. Hopefully, he'd understand. She shook her head. Since when did she want Rider to understand her and her motives?

"You must have a lot on your mind, mija. I can practically hear you thinking from over here."

Jalissa swallowed her last bite and placed her bowl on the small bistro-style table. "Rider took me to meet his family yesterday."

Mom's eyebrows rose. "Family, mija?"

"Not like that." Her cheeks heated. "Just as friends. He's already met you and the Tuckers. It seemed right to meet his uncle and aunt. They were a big part of his high school life."

"I take it something happened, then?" At Jalissa's nod, Mamí continued. "Did they not like you?"

"It wasn't that."

"Then what was it?"

Jalissa stared into Mamí's warm brown eyes, shaped exactly like Jalissa's. "Rider's uncle, he's the—" She cleared her throat. "His uncle was the one with Dad. The one who left him…" Her voice cracked as tears sprang to her eyes.

Mamí gasped. "You are certain?"

"Yes." Jalissa nodded. "He said so himself."

"Did he explain what happened? Offer *any* justifications?"

"I didn't stick around to find out." But wasn't that like her mother to want the extra details?

Her mother studied her, gaze tightening with worry. "You had a panic attack, didn't you?" The words were flat, devoid of emotion, as if Mamí worried being overly concerned would tip Jalissa right over.

"Yes, but Rider talked me through it." Not to mention Flo. She peered down at man's—*woman's*—best friend.

"This Rider, he has become important to you?"

"No." She paused. "I mean, we're friends, but that's all." All there could ever be. Jalissa wasn't cut out for more. She could only imagine the many panic attacks she'd have wondering if he'd come home after his shift.

"Are you sure there's not more?" Her mother leaned forward, brow furrowed with scrutiny.

Jalissa wanted to shrink back in her seat, but that would give her mother ammunition to believe there was something there. Besides… "There can't be more. Didn't you just hear what I said about his uncle? Don't you remember the hurt and pain we went through?"

"Ah, mija, that has nothing to do with you and Rider."

How could it not? She couldn't go over to the Riders' home knowing Jay was the reason Jalissa didn't have a father. That stress and awkwardness would ruin any chance at a relationship she and Rider could have. *Not* that she was thinking those thoughts.

She wouldn't. What-ifs were a dangerous game to play. They ruined either present peace or future hopes. Jalissa was a firm believer in living in the present, and thinking that she and Rider could have any type of relationship outside of friendship was delusional.

"It doesn't matter. We're just friends." And she would keep saying that until it cemented into her thoughts.

"At least that has changed. I remember when you vehemently denied having any cordial feelings toward him at all."

"That's because he was always antagonizing me."

"Are you sure it wasn't the other way around?"

Jalissa laughed. "What can I say? I'm a force of nature."

"And have been since you were born." Mamí smiled, a faraway look in her eyes. "Always making your displeasure known the instant you felt it. I need to talk to him. Rider's uncle."

Jalissa's stomach knotted. "I'll see to it."

"Gracias, mija. You're a good daughter." Mamí leaned forward and wrapped Jalissa in a hug. "I know the news must have been a shock, but it wasn't to God." She pulled back. "Remember that. Everything you think you know,

God knows the truth of the matter. So if, *if* you wanted to date Rider, your relationship with his family will fall under God's sovereignty. He and only He knows if it truly is an issue or not."

Jalissa wanted to object but kept quiet. When her mother spouted spiritual wisdom, she really didn't expect Jalissa to agree or disagree. Instead, she always hoped Jalissa would listen, then discuss it with God. Usually Jalissa nodded like a dutiful daughter and argued silently in her head.

She spoke up. "But what about the pain of losing someone? Of being disappointed by their constant absence?"

She remembered all the times Mamí had been disappointed. Remembered the ache of seeing that coffin lower. What if she let Rider in and had to deal with a repeat in history?

"Mija, you can't be afraid of livin' because of what-ifs. You may miss out on many great blessings. If I had been afraid of marrying a firefighter, I would not be sitting with you today." Mamí stroked her hair. "I have no regrets, mija." She pointed to the Bluebonnet Fire department flag hanging from the awning. "None. I had a love that's lasted a lifetime and a family in you and the Tuckers."

Tears sprang to Jalissa's eyes. Thinking of her animosity toward firefighters, Jay and everything Mamí had just said made her head ache. "It's too much."

"Then give it to God. Give everything to Him. The tiny details, the big dreams. He'll know what to do." Mamí stood. "Don't forget God works all things for good."

"I won't."

All the way home, Jalissa thought about her conversation with her mother. Could Jay's involvement in her father's death really work out for good? Her mind couldn't wrap around the concept, and her brain shouted in protest at the mere idea.

After she arrived home and filled Flo's bowl, Jalissa

pulled her cell phone out of her back pocket. Her finger hovered over the text icon. Maybe she should call Rider instead, let him know she was okay, then ask him to arrange for her mom to talk to Jay. Yet the idea of trying to navigate the conversation live sent a wave of apprehension through her. She pressed the icon then scrolled to his name.

Jalissa: My mom would like to talk to your uncle.

Rider: Absolutely. He offered and I was going to pass that info along to you.

Jalissa: Consider it passed. Let me know when he can meet.

Rider: Anytime. Just text me your mom's availability.

An ellipsis appeared on her screen. She tapped her foot, waiting for him to reply. When the message posted, she scoffed.

Rider: Are you okay?

He must have deleted some texts. There's no way it had taken him that long to type three words out.

Jalissa: I will be.

Rider: Anything I can do to help?

Jalissa: Set up the meeting for my mom.

Rider: Will do.

She bit her lip, staring at those two words. Had she been too abrupt? Hurt his feelings? Her fingers flew across the qwerty keyboard.

Jalissa: Thank you for checking on me.

Rider: Anytime.

Her lips curved into a smile, and she set down her phone before she could do something silly, like continue to text him.

With each exhale, Rider curled the dumbbells. He loved the fact that the firehouse had a weight room. It helped him pass the time or, in this case, work out some frustration. He'd been thinking through everything his uncle had shared, as well as Jalissa's request for her mom to talk to Jay. He prayed that meant her mom was handling the revelation well, but he honestly didn't know.

Jalissa was like a vault—not sharing much. The only thing she'd discussed in detail was next week's fund-raiser. Everything was set up. He'd been praying they would pull in a lot of money from the dinner-auction event.

Rider couldn't wait for it to all be over so *fund-raising* would no longer be a frequent vocabulary word he used. It was odd, constantly thinking of ways to bring in more money. He'd told Jalissa they needed to come up with avenues the town could use to keep an influx of cash coming in so no one had to worry about being put on the chopping block again. Maybe ask the mayor to set up a fund-raising committee that didn't involve him and Jalissa.

Not that he didn't appreciate working with her. It had helped him see behind the facade she presented to everyone. But as much as Rider had learned about her, he couldn't help but feel like there were more layers to peel back. Why wouldn't she let him in?

He blew out a breath and set the weights down.

"Are you done, or are you going to mess up the punching bag next?" Omar asked, leaning against the door frame.

Rider eyed the object in question. "That's not a bad idea."

Omar chuckled. "Women problems?"

"I wish."

"What?" Omar's eyebrows rose. "What could be so bad that you'd rather deal with the complications of life with a woman?"

"Do you regret marrying Trinity?"

"Not at all. I love her. My life is better with her."

See! That was what he was beginning to understand. Jalissa was a fighter, and something told him if she gave him a chance, he wouldn't be whining about another heartbreak. "Yet you say life with women brings complications."

"It does. But that's life." Omar grinned. "It just so happens she's worth it."

"Exactly. If I had a problem with a woman, maybe it's because she's worth it." If Rider could get Jalissa to trust him, he had a feeling he'd be experiencing the same happiness as Omar.

"Then what's up? What's going on?"

Rider recapped the events from two days ago. Omar sat quietly on the weight bench until Rider finished. Rider wiped at his forehead with the white towel around his neck.

"I don't know what to think. I don't know if I should beg Jalissa's forgiveness for something my uncle did." He paused, wondering if he should admit out loud the thoughts rolling around in his mind. "And I don't know if that prevents me from having any chance with her."

"Whoa. I didn't see that coming." Omar shook his head, a wry grin on his face. "But Trinity called it."

"Really?" Rider wasn't sure how he felt about Omar and Trinity talking about his supposed love life.

"Yeah. She mentioned the idea when we went bowling last year."

"Ah."

"So you want to date Jalissa?"

Now that the question was out there, Rider could be honest. "Yes. It took a while for her to stop disliking me and even more to become friends. Just when I thought we were in a good position, Uncle Jay drops a hand grenade into our relationship. Now I feel like everything's in pieces and she'll barricade me further from her life."

"Have you talked to her? Told her how you feel?"

"She asked for space."

"How long has it been since then?"

Did texting count? "I haven't seen her in two days." And it had been a long two days.

Omar's mouth twisted with thought. "I don't know Jalissa very well, and I think she likes it that way. So honestly, you'd be a better judge on when you can reengage. I don't think asking Trinity would be helpful, because then you enter the realm of gossiping."

"Not seeking wisdom?"

"You might be asking Trinity to break some confidences. I mean, you did get Trinity to help her. Maybe that's all you need to do to let her know you care."

Rider nodded, but he didn't like the answer. How could Jalissa know he cared when he'd just now figured it out? "I'll think about what you said."

"Sure. And I'll be praying this meeting with your uncle goes well."

Rider had been doing just that since the moment he saw the text from Jalissa. His uncle had readily agreed, but still, what would come of the meeting? Would all parties really receive closure, or would Rider be left to pick up the pieces of heartache and bitterness?

Chapter Twenty-One

The heater blew steadily in Jalissa's face as she navigated the gravel driveway leading to Jay Rider's home. Although October had its warm days, a cold front had come through last night and thrown them straight into fall. Hopefully the sweater she wore would keep the chill of the thirty-degree drop away.

Her conversation with her mother had quieted as soon as Jalissa made the turn off the main road. Now the only sound filling the inside of her hatchback was the crunching of rocks under the tires.

She missed Flo. She'd thought about bringing her companion for moral support, but it seemed pretentious to assume Jay would welcome her four-legged friend again. Especially since Rider wasn't here as a buffer. He'd offered to come and support Jalissa and her mom, but she just couldn't see him yet. It was bad enough they would have to work together for the fund-raiser next week.

Finally, she put the car in Park and turned to face her mom. "You ready?"

"It will be all right, mija. God has worked out the details, hmm?"

"Right," Jalissa muttered. She wasn't so sure He had—nevertheless, she'd been praying He would.

I really want this to go well, Lord. I'm not sure I see how it can though. But Rider says You care about the small things, so obviously You know how big this is for us. Please, work out the small details, as Mami believes You will. As I want to believe. Help my unbelief.

Jalissa got out of the car and rounded the front. She opened the latch on the gate, motioning for her mother to go first. Soon they stood on the front porch, and Jalissa's stomach somersaulted as if she'd taken a ride on the tilt o' whirl at the Bluebonnet spring fair.

After knocking, they waited a few moments before someone opened the door. Jay filled the door frame, lines etched in his forehead, as if he was nervous. Was it bad that Jalissa hoped he was? Why should she and Mamí be the only ones in turmoil? Well, just Jalissa—her mother looked cool as a cucumber.

Jalissa cleared her throat. "Mr. Rider, this is my mother, Yesenia Tucker. Mamí, this is Rider's uncle Jay."

"Nice to meet you, Mrs. Tucker." Jay shook Mamí's hand. "Please come in."

They headed for the living room, where Jalissa took a seat next to her mother on the sofa. She willed her leg not to shake or any other part of her body to give a sign of nervousness. She'd done a lot of praying and deep breathing exercises this morning, hoping to stave off another panic attack.

Her mother slid a hand in hers, and Jalissa squeezed it.

"Thank you for having us, Mr. Rider. My daughter told me a little of what you shared with her." Mamí paused.

Lord, please give her the words. Please comfort her.

"I'd like to hear it from you, in private."

"What?" Jalissa stared at her mother. "I have questions, too," she whisper-shouted.

"Mija," her mother murmured, "you need to forgive. But I—" she placed a hand on her chest "—I need to know my husband's last moments. We do not share the same problems. You can talk to Mr. Rider when I am done."

Jalissa nodded, trying to keep the tears at bay. Her mother's tone held no censure, but Jalissa felt convicted all the same.

Jay stood. "We can talk in the backyard, if that's okay?"

"Yes. That will be fine."

Mara walked in. "Oh, I got distracted with a phone call. I'm Mara, Jeremy's aunt." They made another round of introductions, then Jay brought his wife up to speed. As Jay and Jalissa's mother left the room, Mara took a seat on the recliner near Jalissa.

"How are you doing, honey?"

Jalissa shrugged. "I'm not sure I know."

"I've had similar moments." Mara sighed. "There are usually so many emotions going on at once, it's hard to sift through them to answer a seemingly simple question of how you're doing, isn't it?"

"Yes." That was exactly it. How could she admit how angry she was that her mother and Jay seemed to have come out of the event unscathed when Jalissa had been tortured by it? Losing her dad had uprooted her and left her altered forever. It wasn't fair to claim her mother hadn't experienced the same thing, but she'd found a peace Jalissa struggled to find to this day.

"I was shocked to discover Jay's involvement in your father's death." Mara's lips turned downward. "It was before I met him and after Jeremy and Rebecca moved to Bluebonnet. He kept this closely guarded." Mara met Jalissa's eyes. "It's hard to love a person who holds everything so close to the heart."

"I can't imagine. I haven't really had many relationships." Not when she'd been working so hard to prevent the hurt that could ensue.

"Hmm. You seem like the type to hold secrets until you deem someone worthy enough. You may be more like my Jay than you'll ever know."

Her stomach tensed. "Are you saying I could have done something like that?"

"Oh, no." Mara waved her hands. "No. Not at all. I don't mean the Jay of that night. I mean who he is now. It took a lot for him to tell you what happened. Then he did it again when Jeremy came back."

"Rider—I mean, Jeremy—came back? When?" And why? Was he upset on her behalf? Or upset that his uncle wasn't as perfect as he'd assumed?

"That same night. He and Jay went outside and talked for a while. Jay didn't divulge what was said. He's good like that. Likes to hold confidences to ensure people he's a safe place to unload any issues they're having."

A safe place.

How ironic. Her dad had died because Jay wanted to be a hero. Now he was being a hero as some uncertified counselor. Jalissa stared down at her hands, knowing anger would show on every facial feature. The tightness in her jaw clenched her teeth until they felt like they could break from the pressure of her clamping them together. She drew in a breath then exhaled.

One...two...three...four...five...six...

She should have brought Flo. If at least to have something to do with her hands besides popping knuckles and pulling on fingers.

"Are you angry with your husband?" Jalissa bit down on her tongue, mad that she'd asked the one question mulling around since Mara confessed she'd had no prior knowledge of Jay's involvement.

"I was."

Jalissa's head shot up. "Not anymore?" What was it about others that they could so easily forgive offenses? Why was she the only one hung up on the past?

"Now I think I'm more hurt than angry. Hurt he didn't think he could tell me. Hurt he kept this a secret all these years. And I hurt for you and your mom."

"But you forgave him?"

"I did."

"Why?" Her throat ached with unshed tears.

"He's my husband, Jalissa. Not only that, but God calls us to forgive. How could I hold that from Jay if God will not?"

Conviction knocked loud and clear, like the birds singing outside her window on a summer's day. Jalissa had never even attempted to forgive the man who had gotten her father killed. Now that she knew who he was, forgiveness had remained the furthest thing in her mind.

What did that say about her? And what did God think about her attitude?

A tear dropped into her lap, and Jalissa brushed it away.

"It's okay to be angry, Jalissa. It's expected. But the question is, what will you do with that emotion? Will you feed it until it's spread into every crevice of your being, making you unrecognizable to even yourself? Or will you turn it over to God and let Him show you how to respond?"

"I don't know how to do that."

"Then tell Him. He'll take it from there. He's just waiting for you to reach out."

Jalissa nodded, but inside, her thoughts were more complicated than making her head bob up and down. Forgiveness seemed too kind of an act to give someone who had taken everything from her. Who'd made her family smaller and filled her with daily anxiety to battle.

"Thou shalt love thy neighbor as thyself."

Her stomach churned as the Bible verse scrolled in her mind. If she called herself a believer, should being unkind even be in her repertoire of behaviors? Jalissa knew the answer. It was a knowledge that was instinctive, easy, considering how many sermons she'd heard, how many times she'd read the Bible and all the time spent at Vacation Bible School.

But her gut instinct wanted to shout against the command and continue the path she'd been living for the last fifteen years.

* * *

Sometimes one had to take a risk. Rider could only pray showing up at Jalissa's house for a walk wouldn't backfire on him. Pongo stared up at him as if to ask, *where is she?* Rider didn't want to knock again if she had chosen to sleep in but didn't want to walk away if she simply hadn't heard him, either. He rubbed his hands together as he weighed the pros and cons.

Just as he decided to knock again, the door opened.

"Rider?"

"Morning, Jalissa."

Her head jerked in a—nod?—he couldn't tell.

"What are you doing here?"

"I thought we could go for a walk." He slid his hands into his gym shorts pockets.

She studied Pongo, then her gaze flitted to his. "All right. Give me a minute."

His shoulders dropped with relief, and he fought the grin that wanted to emerge. He didn't want to scare her off, because she wore enough caution signs to slow down traffic county-wide.

Rider walked toward the street. "Think she'll open up on our stroll, boy?"

Pongo barked.

"I'll take that as a yes. I need positive thinking right now."

Pongo's tongue lolled out.

The sound of the door shutting pulled him from his one-sided conversation with his dog. He watched as Jalissa and Flo made their way down the walkway. He pulled his foot up behind him, stretching his quad.

"We going to start slow, or do you need to speed walk and get some frustration out?" he asked.

"Let's start slow. I had a rough night, and I'm still waking up."

He dropped his foot. "Did I wake you?" *Great.* Off to a bad start already.

"No. I've been up for a half hour, hoping I'd fall back asleep." She shrugged. "Maybe exercise will clear the cobwebs."

"Then lead the way."

Jalissa started down the street as Rider kept pace. He focused on his footsteps so he wouldn't be tempted to fill the silence right away. But he desperately wanted to know how she was doing, especially since she'd mentioned a bad night's sleep.

"What are your plans for the day?" Jalissa asked.

"Uh… I'm going to see Sean later. He wanted to catch a movie."

"That sounds fun. Is there a good one out?"

Since when did they talk about superficial stuff? Then again, hanging with his SAFE pal was important to him. "No, but the theater has the throwback movies program, where they play old releases for a dollar. We'll go to one of those. Sean will pay for our tickets, and I'll pay for snacks."

"Whose idea was it to split the cost?"

"His, but I offered to buy snacks. Once he realized I'd be paying the most, it was too late for him to argue."

"That was smart of you."

"I can be that sometimes." He winked, mentally patting himself on the back when she blushed.

"Ha."

The sound of their footsteps hitting pavement soothed some of his nervousness. This was Jalissa. They had a good rapport. He didn't have to think the situation to death. If she shot him down when he asked her out, he'd survive.

Will you really? Because he didn't want only one date. He wanted more.

"I heard you talked to your uncle about everything."

He almost stumbled. What was she talking about? "About you and your mom?"

"No. About my father and your uncle's involvement."

"Oh. Yeah." He nodded, on track with her comment. "I went back after dropping you off that night."

Jalissa said nothing for a moment, so when she spoke, it sent goose bumps up Rider's arms. "Was that hard for you?"

"It was, actually." He glanced at her, then faced forward. "I never imagined he'd be involved in something like that. I'm not sure what he told y'all when you spoke, but the person he used to be was very different from the man who helped me through high school."

"Yeah. Your aunt said something similar."

"Do you believe it?"

"Well, you see, my mom wanted to talk to him alone. By the time she was done, I got the feeling he didn't want to talk anymore, so I left."

That wasn't like her. She usually pushed until she got the desired result. "Why didn't you speak with him?"

"I talked to your aunt about emotions and dealing with forgiveness." She shrugged. "I guess I tried to take a step in the right direction. The questions I have won't bring my father back. More than likely, they would just fuel the anger I've been harboring over the years." Jalissa looked at him. "I don't want to be angry anymore."

Rider stopped, stunned by her admission. "You don't?"

"I don't."

This was it. His chance. He cleared his throat. "Even with me?"

She tilted her head. "We're friends now. I stopped being angry with you a while ago."

"Good." He took a step forward. "Because I'd like to take you out on a date."

Jalissa's eyes widened, and she took a step back.

Not a good sign. He paused, forgetting the rest of the

words he'd planned on saying. He'd thought she'd be a little hesitant, but the look on her face spoke measures beyond hesitation.

"I don't think that's a good idea."

"Do you not like me like that?" He hated the insecurity in his voice, reminiscent of his high school years, but he had to know.

"It's not that."

"Then what is it?" He tried to keep his tone calm and even despite the hammering of his heart.

"You put your life on the line every time you answer a call." She gulped. "I can't say yes to a date knowing that. Not to mention my less-than-cordial feelings toward your uncle."

"So now you're judging me based on one firefighter instead of the whole fleet of us?" He winced inwardly. That was a low blow. She'd been honest enough, vulnerable, even. Why did he have to revert back to caveman behavior?

She stepped back. "I'm sorry."

Sorry. Seemed like that was the story of his life. He never measured up and was always found wanting. He swallowed down any retorts. Pongo came up next to him, nudging his hand.

"I think I'll head back home, Jalissa."

"Rider—"

He shook his head, turned around and moved into a sprint. Maybe he could outrun the rest of his feelings if he was fast enough.

Chapter Twenty-Two

Why did things always go wrong at the last minute? Jalissa ended the call and dropped her head into her hands. One of the bachelors had been in a car accident. Overall, he was okay, but he'd suffered a broken leg and was set to have surgery tomorrow. Which meant they were a bachelor short. Whom could she find on such short notice to fill the slot?

The auction was at seven. Jalissa would have to open the community center doors around five to give the teens a chance to decorate. Getting the SAFE kids and the other Bluebonnet teens involved had been a blessing. Plus, it saved on up-front costs.

She opened her notebook full of auction notes. As she scanned the list of people helping and those up for auction, her mind remained empty of solutions.

Lord God, what do I do? I don't have anyone else to call.

She opened her text messages and pulled Rider's name up. Her finger hovered over the keyboard as she remembered the expression on his face when she'd said she wouldn't go on a date. He hadn't been heartbroken, but it was obvious her answer caused enough visceral reaction for him to run away like that. As much as she'd wanted to give him a different answer, she couldn't do that to him or herself. He deserved to be with a person who didn't have any baggage and wouldn't hate someone in his family.

She hadn't heard a word from him the past two days and had been absolutely miserable. Part of her just wanted to say yes, she'd go on a date with him. Anything to get him back in her life. Yet how could she when she was still terrified to lose him?

Well, you don't have him now, do you?

Regardless, she needed to let him know about the minus-one-bachelor situation.

Jalissa: Bachelor #10 was in a car accident. He's okay but needs surgery. Who can fill his spot? Any suggestions?

Rider: I'll do it.

Her mouth dropped. How could he even consider doing that? He wasn't free—

You turned him down. Plus, they'd never actually dated.

Her heart pounded in her chest. Why had she never contemplated how it would feel to see him date someone else? She swallowed.

Jalissa: Fine. That works.

Her fingers flew across the screen, then she sent another message.

Jalissa: Are you sure you want to?

Why did you ask that?

Rider: Do I have a reason not to?

Her head bobbed up and down instinctively while her heart warred. "Why me, Lord? Why did you make my heart melt for a firefighter?"

But the Lord was quiet, and Flo apparently didn't think Jalissa was having a real crisis, as she barely glanced up from her dog bed. Jalissa had to think of the shelter. Of SAFE.

Jalissa: If you want to, I guess not.

Rider: That's not what I meant, and you know it.

Way for him to call her out. But she was firm in her resolve. Rider deserved better than someone afraid of everything.

Jalissa: You don't have a reason not to be bachelor #10.

She winced as the words blinked on the screen, sent and already read by him.

Rider: Then I'll see you tonight to collect my bachelor sign.

Tears gathered in her eyes as she imagined him wearing a sign pinned on his back. One of the teens had thought it would be neat for the bachelors to have them on their suits. The women would wear sashes Miss America–style with their bachelorette numbers.

Jalissa: Thank you.

He replied with a thumbs-up. *A thumbs-up!*

She blew out a breath and got up, pacing back and forth as the implications hit her. Rider was going to be put up for auction. He'd go out on a date with someone who wasn't her.

If he wasn't a firefighter, would you admit the feelings you've been secretly harboring?

She squeezed her eyes shut. It wasn't that simple. The risks of having her heart torn in two and the added involvement of Jay in her past made her feelings all the more complicated.

A knock on her door stopped her pacing. Trinity had said she'd do Jalissa's hair and makeup for tonight, but her friend was meeting her at the community center. So who could be at her door?

She twisted the knob and gasped.

"Sorry. I didn't have your number to call. Your mom told me where you live." Jay Rider looked sheepish. "Hope that's okay."

"Uh, sure." But completely unnerving. Why was he here? "Would you like to come in?"

"Yes, please."

Jalissa pulled the door open wider for him to enter, then closed it behind him and said a quick prayer for guidance. "Um, can I get you something to drink?"

"No, thank you. I just came over to talk for a moment."

"Okay. We can sit in the living room." She motioned for him to follow her.

Her thoughts swam in the vicinity of *why* as they sat.

"I'm sure you're wondering why I'm here."

Yep! "That may be front and center."

He chuckled then rubbed his beard. "We didn't have a chance to talk one-on-one when you and your mom came over. I know you had questions, so I was surprised when you left."

"You looked a little worn from talking with Mamí. I didn't want to pile more on you." She shrugged. "And maybe I didn't think my questions would be beneficial to either one of us."

"I appreciate the grace you've given me."

Had she done something gracious? "Maybe it wasn't grace so much as me trying to prevent anger from over-taking me."

"Well, now that you've had a few days to assess how you feel, what would you like to ask me?"

A question immediately popped into her mind. "Do you regret not obeying the order to stay together?"

"Yes."

"That's it? No elaboration?" What did she want him to do? Get on his knees and beg her for forgiveness?

"I want to be sure I don't make any excuses for my action. Which means, yes, I have regrets. Yes, if given another opportunity, I'd obey. But having fallen so short, that incident showed me the power of God's forgiveness."

And they were back to that. *Forgiveness isn't for the wrongdoer. It's for the wronged. To free them from the oppression of unforgiveness and ensure their heart stays in a state of humility with God.* Jalissa's mom's words washed over her.

They had talked about forgiveness after leaving Jay's house. At the time, Jalissa hadn't understood what her mother meant, but now it all made sense.

"Did you really only come over here to make sure I had my questions answered?" She eyed him skeptically.

"That and I felt like you needed more from me." He paused, rubbing the stubble on his chin. "I'm not exactly sure what, but it was a nudge from God I couldn't disregard."

She sighed. "Thank you." Because God was giving her an opportunity she couldn't ignore. An answer to her prayers. "I think I simply needed to look you in the face and say I forgive you," she said slowly.

Shock flashed in his gray eyes, then his bottom lip trembled. As tears welled in his eyes, matching ones found Jalissa's, and soon they were both silently crying.

"Thank you," they said simultaneously.

Jalissa chuckled, wiping at her face. "Thank you for freeing me from my anger. I'm sorry it took me so long to forgive." And glad God gave her an opportunity to say the words. She needed to say them out loud to really have them sink in.

"I'm not. You blessed me by forgiving me face-to-face."

He stood and offered his hand. Jalissa shook it and smiled, thankful for the lightness in her heart.

"Mind if I say one more thing?" Jay asked.

"Please."

"Living in fear is one of the toughest things to do. I never knew how Mara would react, so I never told her about your father. By God's grace and her faith, she's forgiven me for my secrets. But if I had just trusted God and been up-front, I would have saved myself a world of hurt."

Jalissa bit her lip. "What does that have to do with me?" Shouldn't he be telling this to his wife?

"Don't shut my nephew out because of fear of the what-ifs. Trust in God to see you through anything you need Him to."

Her mouth parted, but words escaped her. Instead, she nodded. All this time she'd thought she was protecting her heart from the pain of loss. But in reality, she'd placed limits on God's goodness and how He wanted her to live.

Rider slid his hands into his suit pockets while Nessa pinned a sign to his back. "Are you sure you're not putting a *kick me* on back there?"

Nessa snorted. "That's so juvenile."

"Aren't you in high school?"

She huffed. "I'm a *senior*. Believe me, I don't go around putting signs on underclassmen. I have too much *class* for that."

"You should be ashamed of that joke."

She giggled, and her face lit into a smile. It was rare for Nessa to actually laugh with him. She was usually rolling her kohl-rimmed eyes and telling him how *old* he was acting.

"It was funny."

"If you say so." He smirked.

"I do." She patted his back. "All done. Now I have to make sure the bachelorettes are ready to go."

"Have you seen Jalissa?"

"No." She shook her head. "But she texted me a few minutes ago and assured me everything was on schedule."

Then why was his stomach in knots? Oh, yeah, because he'd agreed to be a bachelor when he didn't have the heart to date anyone but Jalissa. He ran a hand down his face.

He couldn't back out now. Everyone was here and ready to bid. The city needed his participation. Thus far, they'd only managed to raise five thousand from the other fund-raisers.

God, please let this go well. Please help us save all the programs. Because as it was, only one of theirs would be safe from the proverbial chopping block.

He hoped the community would show up in droves. Jalissa had even traded a favor with someone at the local radio station to get them to mention the auction. People were now arriving for the dinner portion. Hopefully the homemade meal Jalissa's mom had overseen would satisfy them.

Rider went to the curtain sequestering the contenders from the partygoers. Everyone was dressed up in their finest. The teens walked around with serving trays, placing plates for the guests. He was really proud of the Bluebonnet teens. They'd done the majority of the work to save the town. It gave him a hope for the future.

His phone chimed, and he pulled it out of his suit pocket.

Jalissa: Ready to kick this off?

Rider: Where are you?

Jalissa: Trinity's doing the finishing touches on my hair.

Rider: The contestants are ready, so whenever you want to start the auction, go for it.

Jalissa had decided to be the MC, but right now he wished she hadn't so he could speak to her. Assure her this auction date meant nothing. Because even though she hadn't chosen him, Rider finally realized it wasn't because she didn't want to. She had real fears, and he had to understand that *and* respect that if he wanted her to give him the chance he was praying for.

Jalissa: Great. Give me a couple of minutes.

Rider clapped his hands to get everyone's attention. He relayed the start time and that the women would go first. That had been Jalissa's idea as well. He was merely along for the ride at this point.

He went back behind the curtain. Soon he heard Jalissa's voice over the microphone, and he motioned for bachelorette number one to step up to the stage. Jalissa called her name, and the woman parted the curtains.

Rider listened as Jalissa gave a little background on Brittany and how she was a first-grade teacher at Bluebonnet Elementary. Then she laid out the rules before emphasizing how the money would benefit the city programs like the shelter and SAFE.

"Your money will go directly to the city council to ensure the programs are funded through the next fiscal year. If we make enough to cover more than one program and more than one fiscal year, all the better. The person with the highest bid will win a date with the bachelor or bachelorette, who has agreed to pay for the date. You're simply getting the opportunity to meet some wonderful people. Now, who's ready to start bidding on a date with Brittany?"

Rider said a quick prayer.

"I hear a bid of fifty dollars—oh, there's hundred. Can we make it two hundred? Great, gentleman wearing the fedora, I acknowledge your two hundred."

Jalissa continued to narrate until the bids closed at three hundred dollars. Rider smiled. If they could get three hundred for every single bachelor/ette, then they could make at least six thousand dollars. Which would bring the grand total to eleven. SAFE and the shelter would be clear, with a little extra to help another Bluebonnet program.

Belinda had found a few donors for SAFE, but last he checked, the center still needed the city's funding in order to continue. He let out a breath. He would just pray that all the singles up for auction made as much as Brittany—*at least*.

The next bachelorette went for two hundred, and another for four hundred. Rider mentally tallied the money until Jalissa announced that was all the bachelorettes. He wanted to cheer. The women had brought in three thousand dollars, thanks to one of the bachelorettes who had been bidden on for a thousand dollars. They now had a total of eight grand.

"I want to take a brief moment to thank all the Bluebonnet teens who have helped us fund-raise and decorate the community center tonight," he heard Jalissa say. "Citizens of Bluebonnet, I hope you know how good your kids are. You've done a wonderful job of raising them, and I know our future will be blessed with them in charge one day. Let's give them a round of applause."

Rider clapped from backstage, catching the eyes of a few teens who had decided to stay behind and out of the spotlight. "Thank you," he mouthed to them.

Nessa blushed, and the others smiled sheepishly.

"All right, y'all. I hope you're ready for the bachelors."

Rider listened quietly as the same routine happened with the men. After four bachelors, they hit their goal of ten thousand. He wanted to raise a fist in the air. SAFE and the animal shelter were okay.

His phone chimed.

Belinda: I just spoke to someone at the auction. We're set. We don't need the city's funding anymore. Make sure some other programs get the benefit of tonight. Y'all are doing a great thing.

Rider breathed out a thank-you to the Lord.

Rider: Who was it?

Belinda: We'll talk more later. But thank you for all you've done.

Rider: Of course. Anytime.

"And now it's time for bachelor number ten."

His heartbeat sped up at the pronouncement. They were done with the other guys? Rider adjusted his tie, then stepped through the curtains. He blinked. Why was Trinity at the podium? Had something happened to Jalissa?

He wanted to pull out his cell and text Jalissa to make sure she was okay, but Trinity started the bidding. He stared out into the audience, trying not to squint at the bright stage lights.

"One hundred," called out a woman he'd seen at the Beanery.

"I hear your one hundred. Is there a two hundred?"

Another woman raised her hand. Soon the bids were inching toward the four-digit mark.

"Don't forget that Rider has been instrumental in raising money for Bluebonnet," Trinity remarked. "I think that deserves higher bidding, don't you?"

"Two thousand dollars!"

Rider's jaw dropped as Jalissa strode forward, her hand in the air.

"Do I hear two thousand and one? Anyone? No? Gone for two thousand dollars!"

Chapter Twenty-Three

Jalissa closed the doors to the community center and locked them, since the mayor was allowing her to return the keys tomorrow. Now to get out of these heels and relax. But first, a certain conversation needed to happen with a certain someone. One she'd been able to put off since she'd yelled out a sum of two thousand dollars.

Jalissa turned and stared at the man who had just taken a portion of her Hawaii savings. Suddenly she felt unsure that he would be pleased with her little attempt at a grand gesture.

"So, two thousand dollars, huh?" Rider strolled up to her, hands in his suit pockets.

Her pulse raced and she bit her lip. "Too low?"

Rider's brow rose. "More like too much. You could have saved yourself two grand if you'd said yes a couple of days ago."

"True." She bit back a smile. "But a couple of days ago, I was pretty sure that you and I were a bad idea."

Talking with Jay had allowed her to admit her feelings, despite all the time she'd spent ignoring them—suppressing them, even. Once Jay had left and the peace of forgiveness had flooded her heart, Jalissa had asked herself whether or not being with Rider and accepting his job was worth any potential anxiety or panic attack.

Rider stepped onto the sidewalk, and her breath caught at the look in his eyes. Why did he have to look so good in a navy blue suit?

"What happened to change your mind?" he murmured.

"Well, I've been praying, for one."

"Do tell."

She grinned. "Apparently God does care about the little details." And wasn't that a blessing? "He found me a bachelor number ten, helped me forgive Jay and showed me a way to say I'm sorry to the man who captured my heart."

"I have so many questions."

"I may have that many answers."

Rider looked contemplative. "Since when did you start praying to God about the little things? When did you forgive Jay? And two thousand dollars is a big *I'm sorry*. But more importantly, who is this man that's captured your heart?"

Jalissa laughed and stepped forward, reaching for Rider's hand. "His family calls him Jeremy, while I used to call him the bane of my existence."

"Ouch, but understandable." He smirked.

"Is it, though?" She sighed. "I had so much bitterness stored up, I didn't even realize how bad it was until I spoke to Jay this morning and told him I forgave him."

"You drove to his house?" His brows rose.

She shook her head. "He came to mine."

"Looks like I have him to thank for a date with the prettiest woman in Bluebonnet."

"Just Bluebonnet?"

Rider laughed.

"Before we go on a date, I just have to ask you something," Jalissa said.

"Ask me anything."

"Are you sure you can handle my anxiety?"

"Definitely." He tucked a strand of hair behind her ear. "But I'm more worried about you handling my job. Do you still hate firefighters?"

She shook her head. "No. I'm so sorry for the grief I've given you regarding that. I *know* you. I know you're not arrogant or cocky or half the terms I came up with when I was running from my feelings."

Rider's lips curved. "From now on, we'll run together. Every day. Wow, that came out cheesier than I intended."

She grinned. "So cheesy, but I'm charmed regardless."

"I hope so," he murmured. "But we need to find out what kind of story we're going to tell our grandkids one day. I can't let them think their grandma paid two thousand dollars for a date." He cocked his head. "Then again, that'll help them realize how devastatingly handsome I was in my youth. Hard to believe when a man's been hit hard by Father Time."

"Oh, you." She pushed his shoulder, and he wrapped her in his arms. "Oh, that was smooth."

"I have to make sure you're always charmed."

"Hmm, I'm too busy wondering how you think we'll have grandkids to talk to one day."

"Sometimes God lets you see a bit into the future. I'm one hundred percent confident we'll go the distance."

"How can you be so sure?"

"Because I'm not going anywhere."

A breath of air escaped her lips as she looped her arms around his neck, leaning into his strength. "Neither am I."

Rider tightened his hold, and they stood there quietly. Slowly, Rider started swaying side to side as if he heard a sweet melody she wasn't privy to. She laid her head against his chest as he began maneuvering them around the parking lot, singing softly in the stillness.

Jalissa didn't know how long they danced as Rider serenaded her, but she couldn't help but pray the moment never ended.

Rider whistled as he turned into Jalissa's driveway. What a difference time made. Last time they'd gone to a town hall, Jalissa had hated his guts and he'd been worried about

SAFE. Now Jalissa was his girlfriend and SAFE was secure, thanks to the surprise donor from the auction. Turned out Harold, his mom's new fiancé, had felt a nudge from God to give. He hadn't yet told Jalissa. Instead, he'd watch her face when the mayor shared the fund-raising results with the town and told them what programs were safe from the chopping block.

Jalissa walked out of the house just as he placed his truck in Park. He hopped out and raced to the other side to open the door for her.

"I like this side of you." Jalissa grinned impishly.

"What? Me racing to hold doors open for you?"

"Yes. It's a good look on you."

He laughed, then kissed her cheek. "I'll hold all the doors for you if it gets you to smile at me like that."

"You're going to be too good to me, aren't you?" She peered up into his eyes.

His heart turned over in his chest. "No such thing as too good. You deserve my very best, Jalissa Tucker."

Since the night of the auction, they'd gone on countless dates. Well, as he retold it. He figured any time they were together was a date. Jalissa said it only counted if they went out somewhere for the purpose of having fun and getting to know each other. In her estimation, they'd been on ten dates. Rider chose not to count since he planned on being with her until God called him home.

Of course, she shied away from talk like that. Rider figured he had months, if not years, for her to catch up to his way of thinking. Good thing he wasn't in a hurry. Being able to call her his girlfriend was enough. He was certain her title would change to fiancée, then wife, eventually.

They made it to the town hall just as the mayor called the meeting to order.

"I'm sure everyone's main concern is how successful the fund-raisers were." The mayor peered over his glasses, gazing at them in the back row. "Jalissa Tucker and Jeremy Rider worked hard as the first-ever town fund-raising committee. Under their suggestion and the approval of our accountant, we have decided to make this a permanent committee. We've already had some volunteers step up to continue their good work, as they will be stepping down and letting someone else take the reins."

Applause stalled the mayor. He waited for everyone to quiet before continuing. "Rider has informed us that SAFE no longer needs city funding. Thus, the funds we raised will be split with the rest of the programs that were going to be defunded or have their funds decreased."

Jalissa grabbed his hand. "What is he talking about?"

He winked. "Shh, he's speaking."

"After the auction, we had multiple private donors come forward. They wanted to help our town prosper. Together with their donations and the funds raised by Jalissa and Jeremy, we gained a total of thirty thousand dollars."

"What?" Jalissa cried.

Rider's mouth dropped. Someone other than Harold had donated? Rider hoped God blessed them all for blessing Bluebonnet.

"Yes, yes, it's a wonderful thing." The mayor motioned for the crowd to quiet down.

"I don't understand what's happening," Jalissa whispered.

Rider took her hand, got up and tugged her toward the exit.

"Why didn't you tell me SAFE didn't need the money?" Jalissa asked once they were outside.

"I thought it would make a good surprise."

"It does. But how long have you known?"

Was she mad at him? Would this be their first fight as a couple? "Since the night of the auction. I found out right before I stepped onto the stage to be bidden on." And the shock of her bid still brought a smile to his face. "I made sure to let the mayor know to take SAFE off the list. I knew at that point the shelter would be fine and some of the other programs would benefit from our efforts."

She looped her arms around his neck. "How did I get so blessed?" she murmured.

He wrapped his arms around her, loving how she fit perfectly. "If you're blessed, then I'm favored. I'm pretty sure I got the better end of the deal."

"I love you, Jeremy Rider," she blurted. She slapped a hand over her mouth and stepped back.

He gently pulled her back where she belonged. "No takebacks." He lowered his head to her forehead. "Besides, I've been wanting to say I love you for the longest."

"Really?" she asked softly.

"Really." He leaned down and pressed his lips to hers.

She sighed against his lips before returning his affection.

At the start of all this, Rider never would have imagined that he'd happily enter a relationship with Jalissa Tucker. He couldn't be happier that God knew better than Rider and had much, much better plans.

Epilogue

One year later

The sound of their feet pounding the pavement brought a smile to Jalissa's face. She looked at Rider, and her grin widened as she found him staring back at her.

"What?" she asked.

"Nothing. Just enjoying this moment."

Jalissa faced forward, knowing she didn't have to respond. They'd hit a stride in their relationship where words weren't always necessary. The comfort of companionship and assurance of love between them was enough.

"Do you know this is one of my favorite things to do with you?" Rider asked.

"Running?" She cast an incredulous look his way. Surely their dates were a lot more enjoyable then exercising.

"Yes. We don't have to ask the other to slow down or speed up. We just instinctively know when we need to keep pace with one another."

Jalissa slowed, pondering his comment. He was right. Since they'd started dating, they'd never asked one another to change their pace. It was just something the other adjusted for instinctively.

She sped up, then turned to run backward, Rider still studying her. "What are you getting at?" she asked. It sounded like he was leading up to something.

He stopped, and she followed suit, watching as he took a couple of steps to lessen the gap.

"I think our relationship is like that as well. We're in

tune with one another." Rider motioned to her, because she'd taken a few steps forward to lessen the gap even more.

"Do you think that's a bad thing?" Because he was starting to worry her. What was the point of this conversation?

"Not at all." He gave her that half tilt to the lips that made her heart swoon.

In the past, she would've called it a smirk. Now she looked for ways to widen his half smile.

"But it does make me wonder," Rider continued, "if we'll ever surprise each other." He took her hands in his.

"Of course we will. It's us." She smiled, relief flooding her. He was merely concerned with making her happy. Well, himself included. "Besides, when I brought you Manny, you were shocked."

"Yeah, you were asking to raise a puppy with me. Plus, Pongo had already assumed he'd be the only dog in my life."

"See? Surprise," she singsonged.

His blue eyes flitted back and forth as he gazed into her eyes. "Do you really think we'll continue surprising one another?"

"I do. Why? Are you worried?"

He tilted his head to the side. "I don't know." He let go of her hands and pulled something out of his pocket. "It depends on this." Then Rider dropped to one knee.

Jalissa's mouth fell open, but words failed her. Were completely absent as her heart skyrocketed in her chest at the sight in front of her. "Rider…" she whispered.

"Jalissa, I know our relationship had a rocky start. But once we took the time to look below the surface, I can't help but feel like we soared. You make me a better man, and all my dreams have you in the forefront. I love you. Will you marry me?"

"Yes," she rasped as tears streamed down her face. She loved this man so much. And the fact that they could still crack jokes with each other. But this right here—the tender moments when he was most vulnerable—made her love him all the more.

He rose, wrapping his arms around her.

She laid her head against his chest as she squeezed his waist. "I love you so much," she murmured.

"Not as much as I love you," he countered.

"Maybe tomorrow that'll be true."

He chuckled and pulled back. "You didn't even look at the ring."

"Hello! Tears." She wiped her face on the sleeve of her shirt. "Okay. Let me see how you did." She curved her mouth into a playful grin.

"You're going to love it almost as much as me." He flipped open the box.

The round-cut diamond sparkled in the yellow band setting. It was simple but classic. "It's gorgeous."

"I had to get a ring half as beautiful as you."

Her lips curved into the smile. "Such a charmer."

"*Your* charmer."

Jalissa wound her arms around his neck. "Does that mean we'll live a charmed life?"

"That means on days when life kicks us in the gut, we'll pull one another up and lean on God for the rest."

It sounded perfect to her. Rider had shown her how much God wanted to be her strength and confidant. Not only that, he'd been sure to show her how much she could trust him, too. Of course they still had arguments, like every couple, but the grace and forgiveness that flowed afterward was enough for her to know they would handle anything that came their way. Who knew an unlikely alliance would lead to her happy-ever-after?

* * * * *

*If you enjoyed this story,
don't miss Toni Shiloh's next emotional romance,
available later this year from Love Inspired!*

*Find more great reads at
www.LoveInspired.com.*

Dear Reader,

I want to thank all of you who reached out to me and asked for Jalissa and Rider's story. I hope you enjoyed their journey.

Enemies to lovers might be my second-favorite trope. There's a wit and snark that can be seen when the two decide the other couldn't possibly have any redeemable qualities. But then shields are lowered, vulnerability is shared and commonality discovered. Watching all that unfold is one of my favorite parts. Add in the animals, and I thoroughly enjoyed writing this story.

If you suffer from anxiety or panic attacks, know that you're not alone. You can reach out to Crisis Support Services online at https://cssnv.org/ or via their hotline, 1-800-273-8255, twenty-four hours a day, seven days a week, in the event of a crisis, such as an anxiety attack or panic attack.

I hope I did this story justice and that you walk away feeling more connected with people at large. I would love to connect with you. You can find me on Facebook at www.facebook.com/authortonishiloh or via my website http://tonishiloh.com.

Blessings,
Toni

COMING NEXT MONTH FROM
Love Inspired

IN LOVE WITH THE AMISH NANNY
by Rebecca Kertz

Still grieving her fiancé's death, Katie Mast is not interested in finding a new husband—even if the matchmaker believes widower Micah Bontrager and his three children are perfect for her. But when Katie agrees to nanny the little ones, could this arrangement lead to a life—and love—she never thought could exist again?

THEIR MAKE-BELIEVE MATCH
by Jackie Stef

Irrepressible Sadie Stolzfus refuses to wed someone who doesn't understand her. To avoid an arranged marriage, she finds the perfect pretend beau in handsome but heartbroken Isaac Hostetler. Spending time with Sadie helps Isaac avoid matchmaking pressure—and handle a difficult loss. But can they really be sure their convenient courtship isn't the real thing?

THE COWBOY'S JOURNEY HOME
K-9 Companions • by Linda Goodnight

Medically discharged from the military, Yates Trudeau and his ex-military dog, Justice, return to the family ranch vowing to make amends—and keep his prognosis hidden. Only civilian life means facing reporter Laurel Maxwell, the woman he left behind but never forgot. When she learns the truth, will she risk her heart for an uncertain future?

CLAIMING HER TEXAS FAMILY
Cowboys of Diamondback Ranch • by Jolene Navarro

After her marriage publicly falls apart, single mom Abigail Dixon has nowhere to go—except to the family she thinks abandoned her as a child. Not ready to confront the past, Abigail keeps her identity a secret from everyone but handsome sheriff Hudson Menchaca. Can he reunite a broken family...without losing his heart?

THE SECRET BETWEEN THEM
Widow's Peak Creek • by Susanne Dietze

In her mother's hometown, Harper Price is sure she'll finally learn about the grandfather and father she never knew. But that means working with local lawyer and single dad Joel Morgan. Winning his and his daughter's trust is Harper's first challenge...but not her last as her quest reveals shocking truths.

EMBRACING HIS PAST
by Christina Miller

Stunned to learn he has an adult son, widower Harrison Mitchell uproots his life and moves to Natchez, Mississippi, to find him. But Harrison's hit with another surprise: his new boss, Anise Armstrong, is his son's adoptive mother. Now he must prove he deserves to be a father...and possibly a husband.

LOOK FOR THESE AND OTHER LOVE INSPIRED BOOKS WHEREVER BOOKS ARE SOLD, INCLUDING MOST BOOKSTORES, SUPERMARKETS, DISCOUNT STORES AND DRUGSTORES.

LICNM0622